Algonquin Indian Tales

Egerton R. Young

Contents

ALGONQUIN INDIAN TALES

BY

Egerton R. Young

CHIEF BIG CANOE'S LETTER

GEORGINA ISLAND, LAKE SIMCOE.
REV. EGERTON R. YOUNG.

DEAR FRIEND: Your book of stories gathered from among my tribe has very much pleased me. The reading of them brings up the days of long time ago when I was a boy and heard our old people tell these tales in the wigwams and at the camp fire.

I am very glad that you are in this way saving them from being forgotten, and I am sure that many people will be glad to read them.

With best wishes, KECHE CHEMON (Charles Big Canoe), Chief of the Ojibways.

INTRODUCTORY NOTE

In all ages, from the remotest antiquity, the story-teller has flourished. Evidences of his existence are to be found among the most ancient monuments and writings in the Orient. In Egypt, Nineveh, Babylon, and other ancient lands he flourished, and in the homes of the noblest he was ever an honored guest.

The oldest collection of folklore stories or myths now in existence is of East Indian origin and is preserved in the Sanskrit. The collection is called *Hitopadesa*, and the author was Veshnoo Sarma. Of this collection, Sir William Jones, the great Orientalist, wrote, "The fables of Veshnoo are the most beautiful, if not the most ancient, collection of apologues in the world." As far back as the sixth century translations were made from them.

The same love for myths and legends obtains to-day in those Oriental lands. There, where the ancient and historic so stubbornly resist any change--in Persia, India, China, and indeed all over that venerable East--the man who can recite the ancient apologues or legends of the past can always secure an audience and command the closest attention.

While the general impression is that the recital of these old myths and legends among Oriental nations was for the mere pastime of the crowds, it is well to bear in mind that many of them were used as a means to convey great truths or to reprove error. Hence the recital of them was not confined to a merely inquisitive audience that desired to be amused. We have a good example of this in the case of the recital by Jotham, as recorded in the book of Judges, of the legend of the gathering of the trees for the purpose of having one of them anointed king over the rest. Of this legend Dr. Adam Clarke, the commentator, says, "This is the oldest and, without exception, the best fable or apologue in the world."

The despotic nature of the governments of those Oriental nations caused the people often to use the fable or myth as an indirect way to reprove or censure when it would not have been safe to have used a direct form of speech. The result was that it attained a higher degree of perfection there than among any other people. An excellent example is Nathan's reproof of David by the recital of the fable of the poor man's ewe lamb.

The red Indians of America have justly been famous for their myths and legends. We have never heard of a tribe that did not have a store of them. Even the hardy Eskimo in his igloo of ice is surprisingly rich in folklore stories. A present of a knife or some other trifle that he desires will cause him to talk by the hour to his guest, whether he be the daring trader or adventurous explorer, on the traditions that have come down to him. The interchange of visits between the northern Indians and the Eskimos has resulted in the discovery that quite a number of the myths recited in Indian wigwams are in a measure, if not wholly, of Eskimo origin. On the other hand, the Eskimo has not failed to utilize and incorporate into his own rich store some that are undoubtedly of Indian origin.

For thirty years or more we have been gathering up these myths and legends. Sometimes a brief sentence or two of one would be heard in some wigwam--just enough to excite curiosity--then years would elapse ere the whole story could be secured. As the tribes had no written language, and the Indians had to depend entirely upon their memory, it is not to be wondered at that there were, at times, great divergences in the recital of even the most familiar of their stories. We have heard the same legend given by several story-tellers and no two agreed in many particulars. Others, however, were told with very slight differences.

We have adopted the course of recording what seemed to us the most natural version and most in harmony with the instincts and characteristics of the pure Indian. The close scientific student of Indian folklore will see that we have softened some expressions and eliminated some details that were non-essential. The crude Indian languages, while absolutely free from blasphemy, cannot always be literally translated. ***Verbum sat sapienti***.

The method we have adopted, in the presentation of these myths and legends in connection with the chatter and remarks of our little ones, while unusual, will, we trust, prove attractive and interesting. We have endeavored to make it a book for all classes. Here are some old myths in new settings, and here are some, we venture to think, that have never before been seen in English dress. These will interest the student of such subjects, while the general style of the book will, we hope, make it attractive to young readers.

Nanahboozhoo, the personage who occupies the principal part in these myths, is the most widely known of all those beings of supposed miraculous birth who played such prominent parts in Indian legends. He does not seem to have been claimed by any one particular tribe. Doubtless legends of him were transmitted down from the time when the division of tribes had not so extensively taken place; when perhaps the Algonquin, now so subdivided, was one great tribe, speaking one language.

The variety of names by which he is known is accounted for by these tribal divisions and the rapid changes which took place in the language owing to its having no written form to maintain its unity.

What his original name was, when legends about him first began to be told, is of course unknown. However, since the white race began to gather up and record these Indian myths he has been known as Misha-wabus, Manabush, Jous-ke-ha, Messou, Manabozho, Nanahboozhoo, Hiawatha, Chiabo, Singua-sew--and even some other names have been heard. We have given him in this volume the name of Nanahboozhoo as that was the one most frequently used by the Indians among whom we lived or visited.

There is more unanimity about his origin, among the tribes, than about his name. The almost universal report is that he was the son of Mudjekeewis, the West Wind. His mother was Wenonah, the daughter of Nokomis.

The author desires very gratefully to record his indebtedness, for assistance or hints received in the pleasant work of here clustering these Indian folklore stories, to many friends, among them such Indian missionaries as Revs. Peter Jones, John Sunday, Henry Steinham, Allan Salt, and also to his Indian friends and comrades at many a camp fire and in many a wigwam. He also wishes in this way to express his appreciation of and indebtedness to the admirable Reports of the Smithsonian Institution. He has there obtained verification of and fuller information concerning many an almost forgotten legend.

In regard to a number of the finest of the photographic illustrations in the volume the author gratefully acknowledges his obligations to the Canada Pacific Rail-way Company, without whose assistance it would have been impossible to reach many of the sublime and romantic places here portrayed; until very recently known only to the adventurous red Indian hunter, but now brought within the reach of any enterprising tourist.

CHAPTER I.

The Children Carried Off by the Indians--The Feast in the Wigwam--
Souwanas, the Story-teller--Nanahboozhoo, the Indian Myth--How the
Wolves Stole His Dinner, and Why the Birch Tree Bark is Scarred--Why
the Raccoon has Rings on His Tail.

Without even knocking at the door there noiselessly entered our northern home two large, unhandsome Indians. They paid not the slightest attention to the grown-up palefaces present, but in their ghostly way marched across the room to the corner where the two little children were playing on the floor. Quickly but gently picking them up they swung them to their shoulders, and then, without a word of salutation or even a glance at the parents, they noiselessly passed out of that narrow door and disappeared in the virgin forest. They were pagan Saulteaux, by name Souwanas and Jakoos.

The Indian names by which these two children were called by the natives were "Sagastaookemou," which means the "Sunrise Gentleman," and "Minnehaha," "Laughing Waters."

To the wigwam of Souwanas, "South Wind," these children were being carried. They had no fear of these big Indians, though the boy was only six years old, and his little sister but four. They had learned to look with laughing eyes even into the fiercest and ugliest of these red faces and had made them their friends.

So even now, while being carried away among the dense trees, they merrily laughed and shouted to each other. The bright patches of sunshine on the ground, the singing birds, and the few brilliant-hued summer flowers, brought forth their exclamations of delight, while all the time the grave, silent Indians hurried them on deeper and deeper into the forest. Yet carefully they guarded their precious loads, and as the antlered deer in passing through the thick woods and under the low branches never strike trunk or bough, so these sons of the forest glided swiftly on without allowing any hurt to come to the children of the paleface, even if at times the faint trail led them over slippery rocks and under low intertwining branches.

The wigwam of Souwanas was pitched in a beautiful spot at the edge of the great forest near the sandy, rocky eastern shore of Lake Winnipeg. This great lake is well called The Sea, which is the meaning of its Indian name. It is about as long as Lakes Ontario and Erie combined and in some places is eighty miles wide.

At the entrance of the wigwam, which was made of a couple of tanned reindeerskins, the children were carefully lifted down from the men's shoulders and then taken into this Indian abode. Coming in suddenly from the bright sunshine it was some time before they could see distinctly. The door flap of deerskin had dropped like a curtain behind them. All the light there was came in through the hole in the top, where the poles of the wigwam crossed each other. Presently, however, they were able to see a circle of Indian children gathered around a small fire that smoldered on the ground in the center of the tent. It was now in the pleasant summer time, but the fire was needed for something else than warmth, as the little Sagastao and Minnehaha discovered before long. They were soon seated in the circle with the red children, who, young though they were, were a wee bit startled at seeing these little palefaces. The white children, however, simply laughed with glee. This outward demonstration seemed very improper to the silent red children, who were taught to refrain from expressions of their gladness or sorrow.

The Indians had brought the white children for a characteristic reason. They had said among themselves, "If the white father and mother love us as they say they do we will test them by taking away their children without asking permission." They also wished to show their own love for the children, and so had really brought them to a children's feast.

It was perhaps as queer a tea party as you ever heard of. There was no table on which to put the good things prepared for the feast. No plates, no cups and saucers, no knives, no spoons, not even a chair! There were no cakes, no tarts, no jam, no pies, not even any bread and butter!

"Well, what a feast!" you say. "Without any place to sit, or good things to eat!" Not too fast! There were both of these. There was the lap of mother earth, and so down on the ground, with bearskins and deerskins on it for rugs, the children sat. Then the deerskin door was again opened and in came Indians with birch-bark dishes, called **rogans**, in which were nicely prepared wild ducks, rabbits, and partridges. But as they were uncooked they could not yet be eaten by the now expectant, hungry children.

Then began the preparation of the feast. Some of the Indians added dry wood to the fire until there was a hot, smokeless blaze. Others took out their sharp hunting knives and cleverly cut up the ducks, rabbits, and partridges. Then these pieces were spitted on the ends of sharp points of hard wood and skillfully broiled or toasted in the hot flames. As fast as the dainty bits of meat were cooked and a little cooled they were given to the children in their fingers, and in that way the little ones had their feast.

Now, please don't turn up your noses at such a feast. Think of it: out in a wigwam in the lovely forest, where the wild birds sing and the squirrels chatter, where is heard the music of the waves playing on the shore but a few yards away, with great friendly Indians as your waiters! The very air of that northern summer gives you an appetite ready for anything.

Those little people, red and white, soon became the jolliest of friends, and as the white children could speak the Indian language as well as their own they were soon all chattering away most merrily while they daintily picked the bones. Of course this way of eating was hard upon their hands, faces, and clothing, but what healthy child ever gave a second thought--if a first--to any of these things?

After a time this feast, as all feasts must, came to an end. Then the question was, "What shall we do next for the children?" for the whole day had been planned by the grown-up Indians for the entertainment of the little people. Canoes had been collected on the shore of Winnipeg, handy if it should be decided that they all should go for an afternoon outing on the water. However, Souwanas, who had gone out to look at the sky and observe the winds and waves, now came in and reported that he thought they would better put off the canoe trip to some time when the lake was more calm. It was then suggested that the children be asked what would please them most. The little folks, white and red, were not slow in giving their decision.

"Tell us a story about Nanahboozhoo."

"Who shall be the story-teller?"

There was a hearty call for "Souwanas!"

On coming in from investigating the weather, but a few minutes before, Souwanas had seated himself on a robe and was now enjoying his calumet, or pipe. Stoical though he was, his dark eyes flashed with pleasure at the unanimous call of the children, but, Indianlike, it would have been a great breach of manners if he had let his delight be known. Then, again, Indianlike, it would never have done to have seemed to be in a hurry. The Indian children well knew this, but who ever heard of white children that could sit like statues, grave and dignified, while the story-teller took time to finish smoking a large pipe of tobacco?

So it was in this case. In their wild excitement and eagerness to have the story begin, both Sagastao and Minnehaha sprang up and, rushing toward Souwanas, vied with each other in seeing which could first pluck the half-smoked calumet from his mouth. Such audacity appalled the Indian children and fairly took the breath away from the older Indians. For was not Souwanas a chief, and the calumet almost a sacred thing while between his lips?

Souwanas, however, was greatly delighted. Here was a new experience, and the very boldness of the children of the palefaces was an evidence of their unbounded confidence and love. To little Sagastao the calumet was surrendered, and, with the children cuddled around him, Souwanas began his story:

"Now, you must know that Nanahboozhoo was a queer fellow. He could make himself as tall as a tree or as small as a turtle or snake. Nothing could kill him. He could not be drowned even if dropped hundreds of feet into the lake, nor burned to death even if he tumbled into the fire. He often met with accidents, but he always came up right again and was ready for some other adventure in some new shape. He has left his marks on the rocks and trees, leaves and flowers. Almost anywhere we look we see signs that Nanahboozhoo has been around. As his temper was very uncertain he sometimes caused trouble and injured the appearance of things which were once more beautiful than they are now. But in general he was the friend of our race and worked changes that were for our good.

"One day, as Nanahboozhoo was walking along on a sandy shore, he felt very hungry. It was now in the autumn of the year. As he wandered on he saw an object moving toward him. He had not long to wait before he saw that this object was a great black bear. He pulled up a young tree by the roots and hid himself, preparing to kill the bear when he should come near. When the bear came near Nanahboozhoo made a big jump out of his hiding place and killed the bear with one blow. Then he built a big fire, and having singed all the hair off the bear he cut him up and nicely roasted him. When the meat was cooked Nanahboozhoo cut it up into fine pieces, for he intended to enjoy his feast by eating leisurely.

"While he was thus busy preparing his feast he was annoyed by a strange sound among the tree tops that rubbed together when the wind blew. Nanahboozhoo was very quick-tempered, and as the noise continued he determined to stop it. So he left his feast on the ground and climbed away up one of those trees to the spot where the other pressed against it. He was endeavoring to pull the two great trees apart when one of his hands got caught between them and was firmly held. While struggling to get loose he heard a pack of wolves running toward his bear meat. This made him struggle the harder to get his hand free. The fierce wolves soon scented the food and had a good time devouring it, in spite of the shoutings of Nanahboozhoo.

"When Nanahboozhoo at length got his hand free and came down he found nothing left of his feast but the skull of the bear. He was very angry, not only at the wolves that had eaten his feast but also at the trees that had held him, the great Nanahboozhoo, in so tight a grip. As the wolves had run away he could not, at present, punish them, but he resolved that he would so punish these great birch trees that they would never give him such a squeeze again. So he prepared a great whip and with it he severely thrashed the trees. Up to this time the birch had been the most beautiful of trees. Its great trunk was of the purest white, without any blemish or blotch upon it. But ever since the thrashing Nanahboozhoo gave it it has had to carry the marks of that terrible whipping; and that is why the white birch tree is so covered with scars.

"When Nanahboozhoo had ceased thrashing the trees he found himself so very hungry that he resolved to eat the brains that were in the head of the bear, that had been overlooked by the wolves. However, he found the skull very hard. So he transformed himself into a little snake, and in this way got inside of the bear's skull and enjoyed his feast. In fact he enjoyed it too much, for when he was through with his eating he could not get out of the skull, he was so full. However, he was able to roll along, skull and all, but as he could not see where he was going he bumped along in a very erratic manner until at length he tumbled into a big lake and sank at first deep down under the waves.

"When he came up to the surface he just put a part of the head of the bear out of the water, as does the bear when swimming. Then he listened intently. It was not long before Nanahboozhoo heard voices saying:

"'Look! There is a bear swimming. Let us kill him.'"

"So there was a chase on the lake, and it was not long before the Indians came up, in their canoe, and one of them with his stone ax struck the bear's head such a blow that he split open the skull.

"This just suited Nanahboozhoo, and instantly he sprang out and made for the shore.

"Then Nanahboozhoo journeyed on and again he began to feel very hungry. The brains of the bear were not much to one who had had his mind set on eating the whole carcass. It was not long before he met the raccoon awkwardly carrying a birch *rogan* that he had stolen from a couple of blind men. Seeing the merry smile on the raccoon's face, Nanahboozhoo bade him a good day, and asked him what was amusing him.

"The raccoon, who did not know that it was Nanahboozhoo with whom he was talking, told him how he obtained the dish. When Nanahboozhoo heard this he was very angry at the raccoon for his heartless trick.

"It seems that there was quite a large settlement of people who had among them a couple of blind men. As these Indians were hunters they had to be on the move a good deal of the time following the game. As the other people were kind-hearted, instead of killing these old blind men, now that they were unable to hunt, they arranged for them a wigwam in a safe, quiet place, near the lake. Then they gave them a kettle and bowl and other necessary things and cut a large pile of wood and placed it close at hand. In order that they might be able to get water for their cooking and yet not stumble into the water their friends fastened a rope, for their guidance, from the door of the wigwam to a post on the edge of the lake.

"The old men were now quite comfortable. Their friends came frequently with abundant supplies of food and the blind men were able to do their own work and were happy together. They divided the day's work so that one day one would be the cook while the other would bring in the wood and go for the water. Next day they would change about. It gave each enough to do, and not too much.

"For a long time the two men lived contented and happy. But it happened that one day the raccoon was out prowling along the shore, looking for something to eat, when he happened to find the end of the rope that was tied to the post at the water's edge.

"Now you must know," said Souwanas, "that, next to the wolverine, the raccoon is the biggest mischief in the woods. He is full of tricks, but he is very cunning and suspicious. So before he interfered with the rope he cautiously followed it up and found that its other end was at the wigwam of these two old blind men. Hearing no noise, he cautiously peered into the wigwam and saw them both sleeping near the fire. There was a smell of something good to eat, and the raccoon decided to wait around to see if he could not get hold of it.

"While he was thus waiting the old men woke up, and one said to the other, 'My brother, I am feeling hungry; let us prepare our dinner.'

"'Very well,' said the other; 'it is your turn to go to the lake for water while I make the fire.'

"When the raccoon heard this he ran down to the lake and quickly untied the rope from the stake and, drawing it back, tied it to a clump of bushes on the land. When the old man with the kettle felt his way along the rope until he reached its end he tried to dip up the water as usual, but all in vain. There was nothing but the dry earth and bushes. Not finding any water he returned to his brother with the sad news that the lake had dried up, and that already bushes were growing where yesterday there was plenty of water. When his brother heard this doleful story he laughed at it, and said:

"'Why, that cannot be possible. No bushes could grow up in such a short time.'

"However his brother declared it was the case, and so the other one said, 'Well, let me go, and see if I can find some water.'

"When the tricky raccoon heard this he hurried back and at once untied the rope from the bushes and refastened it to the post near the water. When the second brother came along he easily found the water, and filling the kettle he returned to the wigwam where he vigorously accused his brother of lying. He, poor fellow, could not understand it and was much perplexed.

"The preparation of their dinner went on, and soon it was ready. There was, however, another one present that the blind men had no suspicion of, and that was the raccoon, who had now noiselessly come into the wigwam and greedily sat watching the preparations. This dinner consisted of eight pieces of meat which, when cooked, were placed in their *rogan*, or wooden bowl. When ready they sat down with this bowl between them and began to eat. Each took a piece of meat, and they talked of various things while they ate.

"The raccoon now noiselessly took four of the pieces of meat out of the bowl and began eating them. Soon one of the men reached into the bowl, to get another piece of meat, and finding only two pieces left, he said:

"'My brother, you must be very hungry, to eat so fast. I have only had one piece of meat, and there are only two left.'

"'I have not taken them,' was the reply, 'but I suspect that you are the greedy one who has eaten them.'

"This made the other brother very angry, and as they thus went on arguing, the raccoon, to make matters worse, and to have, as he told Nanahboozhoo, some more sport with the old blind fellows, hit each of them a smart blow on the face. The poor old men, each believing that the other had struck him, began to fight; and so they upset the *rogan* and lost the rest of their dinner and nearly set the wigwam on fire.

"The raccoon then seized the two remaining pieces of meat and the bowl, and, with shouts of laughter, rushed out of the wigwam. The old men, hearing this, perceived that they had been fooled, and they at once stopped fighting and apologized to each other.

"The raccoon's rascally trick made Nanahboozhoo very angry. Indeed he had had a good deal of trouble to keep from letting the raccoon know who he was. So just as soon as the raccoon had finished he said:

"'I am Nanahboozhoo. Those old blind men are my brothers, and I'll teach you a lesson you will never forget!'

"So he seized the raccoon and killed him, and carried his body back to the tent of the blind men and made out of it a great feast for them, and declared that in future the old raccoons should have to carry as many circles on their tails as pieces of meat that had been stolen out of the *rogan* of the blind men."

"Good for Nanahboozhoo!" shouted Sagastao. "Mr. Raccoon couldn't play any tricks on him. Now tell us another story."

But here Minnehaha interposed.

"I think," said she, "we had better go home now, for father and mother may begin to think they have lost their little ones."

"Let us wait until dark," said Sagastao, "and then Mary won't see our dirty clothes!" For their greasy fingers had soiled them badly.

The wishes of the little girl, however, prevailed, and so it was not long ere the Indian salutations, "Wat cheer! Wat cheer!" were shouted to all, and once more the two children were hoisted upon the shoulders of the big Indians, and in the same manner in which they had been brought to the wigwam in the forenoon they rode home in the beautiful gloaming.

Very tired were they, yet not so weary but that they were able with their little hands to rub some of the paint off the faces of their big stalwart carriers and daub it on their own. The effect was so ludicrous that their merry laughter reached the ears of their expectant parents even before they emerged from the gloom of the forest.

CHAPTER II.

The Children's Return--Indignation of Mary, the Indian Nurse--Her Pathetic History--Her Love for the Children--The Story of Wakonda, and of the Origin of Mosquitoes.

In reaching home the children were quietly received by their parents, who, understanding Indian ways, had no desire to lessen their influence by finding fault with them for carrying off the children. They treated the matter as though it were one of everyday occurrence.

Mary, the Indian nurse, however, did not regard the incident so calmly. When the children were brought back dirty, greasy, bedaubed, and so tired that they could hardly hold up their little heads, her indignation knew no bounds, and as she was perfectly fearless she couched her sentiments in the most vigorous phrases of the expressive Cree language.

The history of Indian Mary was very strange. Indeed there was an incident in her life so sad that from the day of her recovery she was considered to be under the special care of the Good Spirit, so that even the most influential chiefs or hunters had a superstitious fear of showing any temper, or making any bitter retort, no matter what she might say.

Years before this time Mary was the wife of a cruel pagan Indian who bore the English name of Robinson. Although she was slight of figure, and never very strong, he exacted from Mary a great deal of hard work and was vexed and angry if, when heavily burdened with the game he had shot, she did not move as rapidly along on the trail as he did, carrying only his gun and ammunition.

Once, when they were out in the woods some miles from his wigwam, he shot a full-grown deer and ordered her to bring it into the camp on her back. Picking up his gun he started on ahead, and being a large, stalwart man, and moving with

the usual rapidity of the Indians on the homeward trail, he soon reached his wigwam. Unfortunately for him--and, as it turned out, for Mary also--he found some
free-traders[1] at his abode awaiting his return. They had few goods for trade in their
outfit, but they had a keg of fire water, which has ever been the scourge of the Indians.

Robinson informed them of his success in shooting the deer and that it was
even now being brought in. The traders not only purchased what furs Robinson
had on hand but also the two hind quarters of the deer which Mary was bringing
home. Robinson at once began drinking the fire water which he had received as
part payment.

He was naturally irritable, and short-tempered even when sober, but he was
much more so when under the influence of spirituous liquors. The unprincipled
traders, knowing this, and wishing to see him in one of his tantrums, began in a
bantering way to question whether he had really shot a deer, since his wife was so
long in coming with it.

This made him simply furious, and when Mary did at length arrive, laboring
under the two-hundred-pound deer, she was met by her husband now wild with
passion and the white man's fire water. Little suspecting danger she threw the deer
from her shoulders, where it had been supported by the carrying strap across her
forehead. Weary and panting, she turned to go into the wigwam for her skinning
knife, but ere she had gone a dozen steps she was startled by a yell from Robinson
which caused her instantly to turn and face him. The sight that met her eyes was
appalling. Before her stood her husband with an uplifted gleaming ax in his hands
and curses on his tongue. Seeing that there was no chance to fly from him she threw
herself toward him, hoping thereby to escape the blow. She succeeded in saving her
head, but the ax buried itself in her spine.

Mary's piercing screams speedily brought a number of Indians from neighbor-
ing wigwams. When they found poor Mary lying there in agony, with the ax still
imbedded in the bones of her back, their indignation knew no bounds.

Indians, as a rule, have great self-control, but this sight so stirred them that
there was very nearly a lynching. Robinson, now sobered by his fears, clearly
foresaw that terrible would be his punishment, and while the Indians and traders

---

1　Fur buyers who were not agents of the Fur Company.

turned to attend to Mary's wounds the wretched husband stealthily slipped away into the forest and was never again seen there. Rumors, however, at length reached Mary that he had fled away to the distant Kaministiquia River, where for a time he lived, solitary and alone, in a little bark wigwam. One day, when out shooting in his canoe, he was caught in some treacherous rapids and carried over the wild and picturesque Ka-ka-be-ka Falls, about which so many thrilling Indian legends cluster.

For seven years Mary was a helpless invalid. When she did recover her back had so curved that she looked like a hunchback. As she was poor, and utterly unable either to hunt or to fish, we helped her in various ways. She was always grateful for kindness, and in return was very willing to do what she could for us. She was exceedingly clever with her needle, and with a little instruction was soon able to assist with the sewing required. However, what especially won her to us and gave her a permanent place in our home, was her great love and devotion to our little ones.

Little Sagastao was only a few months old when she installed herself as his nurse, and for years she was a most watchful and devoted as well as self-sacrificing guardian of our children in that Northern home. She seemed to live and think solely for them. At times, especially in the matter of parental discipline, there would be collisions between Mary and the mother of the children; for the nurse, with her Indian ideas, could not accept of the position of a disciplined servant, nor could she quietly witness the punishment of children whom she thought absolutely perfect. Hence, if she could not have things exactly as she wanted them, Mary would now and then allow her fiery temper to obtain the mastery, and springing up in a rage and throwing a shawl over her head she would fly out of the house and be gone for days.

Her mistress paid no attention to these outbursts. She well knew that when Mary had cooled down she would return, and it was often amusing to see the way in which she would attract the children's attention to her, peering around tree or corner, and then come meekly walking in with them as though they had only been for a pleasant outing of an hour or so.

"Well, Mary," would be the greeting of her mistress, while Mary's quiet response would be the Indian greeting of, "Wat cheer!"

Then things would go on as usual for perhaps another six months, when Mary would indulge again in one of her tantrums, with the same happy results.

She dressed the children in picturesque Indian costumes--coats, dresses, leggings, moccasins, and other articles of apparel of deer skin, tanned as soft as kid, and beautifully embroidered with silk and bead work. Not a spot could appear upon their garments without Mary's notice, and as she always kept changes ready she was frequently disrobing and dressing them up.

When Souwanas and Jakoos came that morning and picked up the children Mary happened to be in another room. Had she been present she would doubtless have interfered in their movements. As it was, when she missed the children her indignation knew no bounds, and only the most emphatic commands of her mistress restrained her from rushing after them. All day long she had to content herself with muttering her protests while, as usual, she was busily employed with her needle. When, however, the two stalwart Indians returned in the evening with the children on their shoulders the storm broke, and Mary's murmurings, at first mere protests, became loud and furious when the happy children, so tired and dirty, were set down before her. The Indians, knowing of the sad tragedy in Mary's life, would not show anger or even annoyance under her scathing words, but, with the stoical nature of their race, they quietly endured her wrath. This they were much better prepared to do since neither of the parents of the white children seemed in the slightest degree disturbed by their long absence or the tirade of the indignant nurse. With high-bred courtesy they patiently listened to all that Mary had to say, and when the storm had spent itself they turned and noiselessly retired.

The children were worn out with their day's adventure, and their mother intimated that Mary ought at once to bathe them and put them to bed. This, however, did not satisfy Mary. It had become her custom to dress them up in the afternoons and keep them appareled in their brightest costumes during the rest of the day; therefore now the weary children, after being bathed, were again dressed in their best and brought out for inspection and a light supper before retiring. The bath and the supper had so refreshed them that when Mary had tucked them into their beds they were wide awake and asked her to tell them a story. But sleep was what they needed now more than anything else, and she tried to quiet them without any further words, but so thoroughly aroused were they that they declared that if she refused they knew somebody who would be glad to have them visit him again, and that he would tell them lots of beautiful things.

This hint that they might return to the wigwam of Souwanas was too much for Mary, who very freely gave utterance to her sentiments about him. The children gallantly came to the defense of the old Indian and also of Nanahboozhoo, of whom Mary spoke most slightingly, saying that he was a mean fellow who ought to be ashamed of many of his tricks.

"Well," replied Sagastao, "if you will tell us better stories than those Souwanas can tell us about Nanahboozhoo, all right, we will listen to them. But, mind you, we are going to hear his Nanahboozhoo stories too."

"O, indeed," said Mary, with a contemptuous toss of her head, "there are many stories better than those of his old Nanahboozhoo."

"Won't it be fun to see whose stories we like the best, Mary's or Souwanas's!" said Minnehaha, who foresaw an interesting rivalry.

Mary had now committed herself, and so, almost without realizing what it would come to, she found herself pitted against Souwanas, the great story-teller of the tribe. However, being determined that Souwanas should not rob her of the love of the children, she was tempted to begin her story-telling even though the children were exhausted, and so it was that when the lad asked a question Mary was ready.

"Say, Mary," said Sagastao, "the mosquitoes bit us badly to-day. Do you know why it is that there are such troublesome little things? Is there any story about them?"

"Yes. Wakonda, one of the strange spirits, sent them," said Mary, "because a woman was lazy and would not keep the clothes of her husband and children clean and nice."

"Tell us all about it," they both cried out.

Mary quieted them, and began the story.

"Long ago, when the people all dressed in deerskins, there was a man whose name was Pug-a-mah-kon. He was an industrious fellow, and had often to work a good deal in dirty places. The result was that, although he had several suits of clothes, he seemed never to have any clean ones.

"It was the duty of his wife to scrape and clean his garments and wash and resmoke them as often as they needed it. But she neglected her work and would go off gossiping among her neighbors. Her husband was patient with her for a time, but at length, when he heard that Wakonda was coming to pay a visit to the people, to see how they were getting along, he began to bestir himself so as to be decently attired, in clean, handsome apparel, to meet this powerful being, who was able to confer great favors on him, or, if ill-disposed, to injure him greatly.

"He endeavored to get his wife to go to work and remove the dirt that had gathered on his garments. She was so lazy that it was only from fear of a beating that she ever did make any attempt to do as he desired. She took the garments and began to clean them, but she was in a bad humor and did her work in such a slovenly and half-hearted way that there was but very little change for the better after the pretended cleaning.

"When the news was circulated that Wakonda was coming, the husband prepared to dress himself in his best apparel, but great indeed was his anger and disgust when he found that the garments which he had hoped to wear were still disgracefully grimy.

"While the angry husband was chiding the woman for her indolence Wakonda suddenly appeared. To him the man appealed, and asked for his advice in the matter.

"Wakonda quickly responded, and said: 'A lazy, gossiping wife is not only a disgrace to her husband, she is annoying to all around her; and so it will be in this case.'

"Then Wakonda told her husband to take some of the dirt which still clung to his garments, which she was supposed to have cleansed, and to throw it at her. This the man did, and the particles of dirt at once changed into mosquitoes. And so, ever since, especially in the warm days and nights of early summer when the mosquitoes with their singing and stinging come around to trouble us, we are reminded of this lazy, slovenly woman, who was not only a trial to her husband, but by her lack of industry and care brought such a scourge upon all the people."

"Didn't Wakonda do anything else?" murmured the little lad; but that blessed thing called sleep now enfolded both the little ones, and with mutterings of "Nanahboozhoo--Wakonda--Souwanas--Mary"--they were soon far away in childhood's happy dreamland.

CHAPTER III.

More about Mary and the Children--Minnehaha Stung by the Bees--How the Bees Got Their Stings--What Happened to the Bears that Tried to Steal the Honey.

The next morning while Mary was dressing them the children told her of their adventures in the wigwam of the Indians. Mary was really interested, though she pretended to be disgusted at the whole thing, and professed, in her Indian way, to be quite shocked when they both confidentially informed her that they had had such a good time that they were going again even if they had to run away and be whipped for it.

This was terrible news for Mary, and placed her in an awkward position. To tell the parents of the children's resolve was something she would never do, as it might bring down upon them some of the punishment which was quite contrary to her principles. Yet, on the other hand, to let them go and to give no information might cause more trouble than she liked to think of.

Neither could she bear the thought of the two children returning from another day's outing with their neat clothing and pretty faces soiled and dirty. Do as they might, she had never once informed on them, and she had no mind to begin now. She earnestly pleaded with them not to carry out their resolve. The little ones were shrewd enough to see that they had thoroughly alarmed her, and they were in no hurry to surrender the power which they saw they had over her.

Mary never said a word in English. She understood a good deal that others said, but she never expressed herself in other than the Indian language. Hence both little Sagastao and Minnehaha always talked with her in her own tongue.

Minnehaha, seeing Mary's anxiety at their determination to run away to the Indians, thought of compromising the matter by insisting that Mary should tell them more tales. If she would do this they "would not run away very soon;" especially did she emphasize the "very soon." This was hardly satisfactory to Mary, but as it was the best promise she could get she was obliged to consent.

Little Sagastao, who was Mary's favorite, once more unsettled her when he said, "Now, Mary, remember, we have only promised not to run away very soon. That means that we intend to do it some time."

It seems that the little conspirators had talked it all over in the morning in their beds, and had decided how they would get stories out of Mary without really promising not to run away to the wigwam of Souwanas.

The children, being dressed, were taken down by Mary to prayers and breakfast, after which an hour was allowed in summer-time for outdoor amusement before the lessons began. Little Sagastao generally spent his hour, either with his father or some trusty Indian, playing with and watching the gambols of the great dogs, of which not a few were kept at that mission home. Minnehaha was with her mother, and was interested in the bestowal of gifts to the poor widows and children who generally came at that hour.

Owing to the isolated situation of the mission, and the fact that there were no organized schools within hundreds of miles, some hours of the forenoon were devoted to the education of the children in the home. The afternoons, according to the season, were devoted to reading and amusement.

Mary, the nurse, while able to read fluently in the Cree syllabics, had no knowledge of English. As the children's education progressed they wanted to teach Mary. She stubbornly resisted, however, declaring that if they taught her to read English they would want to make her talk it.

The mother noted the unusual expectancy manifested by the children during the day, and on inquiring the reason was promptly informed that Mary had promised to tell them a story, or legend, and "had got to do it."

"Why has she *got* to do it?" said the loving mother, struck with the emphasis which they had placed on the word.

The little mischiefs were cunning enough to see that they had nearly run themselves into trouble, and were wisely silent. Mary also noticed this, and at once her great loyalty to the little folk manifested itself, and quickly turning to her mistress she said, with an emphasis which was quite unusual:

"Mary has promised them a story, and as she always keeps her word she has *got* to tell it."

Saying this she quickly sprang from the floor, where she had been sitting, and taking a child by each hand she marched with them out of the room.

"Hurrah for you, Mary! you saved us that time," said little Sagastao.

Mary would not have been sorry if in some way the parents received an inkling of what was in the minds of the children, yet she had such peculiar ideas that she would never herself be the one to convey that information.

During the brief summer months the pleasantest walks were along the shores of the lake. Many were the cosy little cave-like retreats where Mary often led the children. There, with the sunlit waters before them, and the rippling waves making music at their feet, the old nurse crooned out many an Indian legend or exciting story about the red men of the past. To-day, however, she was perplexed by the attitude of the children and could not select any story that she thought of sufficient interest to divert their minds from Souwanas and Nanahboozhoo. So for a time they wandered on along the pleasant shore, or turned aside to gather the brilliant wild flowers.

A scream of pain from Minnehaha interrupted their pleasure. In gathering some wild lilies she was stung on both hands by some honey bees that were in the flowers. Mary quickly made a batter of clay and bound up the wounded hands in it. Then she sat down and took the child in her lap.

"Naughty bees to sting me like this," said Minnehaha, with tears streaming down her cheeks. "I was not doing them any harm."

"Yes, you were, and so were we all," said the brother. "We were carrying off the flowers from which they get their honey, which is their food."

"Well, they might let us have a few flowers without stinging us," replied Minnehaha.

The intense pain of the stings rapidly abated under Mary's homely but skillful treatment, and as the child still retained her place in Mary's lap she said,

"Can you tell us why such pretty little things as bees have such terrible stings? My hands felt as if they were on fire when I was first stung, and I could not help crying out with the pain."

"Well," said Mary, "there was a time when the bees had no stings, and they were as harmless as the house flies. They were just as industrious as they are now, but they had any amount of trouble in keeping their honey from being stolen from them, for every creature loves it.

"In vain they hid their combs away up in hollow trees and in the clefts of high rocks. The bears, which are very fond of honey, were ever on the lookout for it, and were very clever in getting it when once they found where it was hidden away. Birds with long beaks would suck it out, and even the little squirrels were always stealing it. The result was that whole swarms often starved in the long winters, because all their honey, which is their winter food, was stolen from them. The bees were in danger of being destroyed. They gave up working in great numbers together, and scattered into little companies, and in the most secret places tried to store away a little honey, just enough to keep them alive from season to season. But even these little hives were often discovered and the honey devoured.

"Things had come to such a pass with them that they had almost given up hope of lasting much longer.

"Fortunately for them, word was circulated that Wakonda, the strong spirit-- the one who sent the mosquitoes--was coming around on a tour, to see how everything was progressing. He was greater than even Nanahboozhoo, and was perhaps a relative of his, but he very seldom appeared, or did anything for anyone. However, it happened that he had this year left his beautiful home at Spirit Lake and was journeying through the country, and he was willing to help all who were in real distress.

"So the bees resolved to apply to him for help. Wakonda received them very graciously, and ate heartily of the present of beautiful honey which some of them had made and had succeeded in keeping out of the way of bears and their other enemies.

"When his feast of honey was over he listened to their tales of sorrow and woe. He was indignant when he heard of the numbers of their enemies, and of the persistency of their attacks upon such industrious little creatures.

"For a time Wakonda was uncertain as to the best method to adopt to help them. He dismissed them for that day, and told them to come again on a day he mentioned, saying that by that time he would know just what to do--for help them he would. The bees were so delighted with this news that they could not keep it to themselves but must go and tell their cousins, the wasps and hornets, and even bumblebees.

"When the appointed time arrived the bees were on hand--and so were the wasps, hornets, and bumblebees. Wakonda welcomed the bees most kindly, but was a little suspicious about their visitors, and he asked some sharp questions. But the bees were in such good humor about the help that was coming that they did not refer to the bad habits of their cousins at all. Then Wakonda made a speech to the bees, and told them how much he loved them for their industrious habits, which he wished all creatures had. He praised them for the fact that, instead of idly wasting the summer days, they used them in gathering up food for the long, cold winter.

"Then he proceeded to give them the terrible stings which they have had ever since, and as the wasps and hornets claimed to be their cousins Wakonda was good-natured enough to give them the same sort of weapons. Some people, especially boys, think this was a, great mistake, and would be very glad if Wakonda had refused to give stings to the yellow wasp and the black hornet."

"Well, what happened after the bees got their stings?" said Sagastao.

"A good deal happened," said Mary, "and that very soon. A lot of them, without as much effort to conceal their nest as formerly, selected a tall, hollow tree, and using a big knot hole as the door began secreting their honey in it. They had made the combs, and were now filling them, when along came a couple of bears. These animals, as you have been told, are great honey thieves, but they always had hard work to find where the timid bees had cunningly hid it away, and now they could hardly believe that right here before them was a great swarm of bees filling the air with their buzzing as they flew in and out of the knot hole.

"With saucy assurance they at once began climbing the tree, expecting to be able to put their long paws into that big hole and draw out the combs. But they never reached that knot hole. The noise they made in their climbing alarmed the bees. Out they came in great numbers, and now, instead of flying around in a panic, like so many house flies, and seeing their honey devoured, they at once flew at their enemies, the bears. They stung them on their noses and about their eyes and lips, and indeed in every spot where they could possibly reach them with their terrible new weapons.

"The bears could not make out what the trouble was. They howled with rage and terror, yet they were resolved to get that honey, and still tried to crawl up higher on the tree. But at length the bees mustered in such vast numbers--for those away gathering honey, as they returned, joined in the attack--that the bears became wild with pain and fear, and had to give up their effort and drop to the ground. Even then the bees gave them no peace, and continued to sting them until they were obliged to run into the dark forest for relief.

"Thus it happens now that almost all creatures that bother the bees are similarly treated."

"Well," said Minnehaha, "they need not have stung me because I was picking a few flowers; but, after all, I am glad they have their stings or I suppose we should never have any honey."

"They are not big enough to have much sense," replied Sagastao, "and so they go for everyone that gets in their way."

Mary now carefully removed the clay poultices, which had effectually done their work. A wash followed, in the waters of the lake which rippled at their feet, and soon not the slightest trace of the sting remained. By the time they reached home both pain and tears were well-nigh forgotten.

That evening before the children were sent to bed they overheard Jakoos, who had come to the house with venison to sell, telling in the kitchen a story that he had heard from Souwanas about a naughty fellow, called Maheigan, who tried to capture a beautiful kind-hearted maiden, Waubenoo, and of how Nanahboozhoo thrashed him, and then afterward, because of some naughty children not holding their tongues, Waubenoo was turned into the Whisky Jack.

What the little children overheard had very much excited their curiosity, and so when Mary was putting them to bed they demanded from her the full story.

As this was one of the Saulteaux Indian legends, while Mary was a Cree, she was not familiar with it. She told the children that she knew nothing about it, but this by no means set their curiosity at rest.

CHAPTER IV.

The Love Story of Wakontas--His Test of the Two Maidens--His Choice--
The Transformation of Misticoosis.

A few days later Mary was annoyed by having the children tell her frankly that they did not think she was a first-class story-teller. For if she had been she ought to have been able to answer Minnehaha's question about what Nanahboozhoo did to Maheigan when he tried to catch Waube-noo.

Mary was vexed at herself that she was unable to answer the question, for she well knew that the children would not rest satisfied until they had the story told them by some one, possibly Souwanas himself. Indeed, knowing them so well, she had fully resolved to post herself from one of the noted story-tellers who have all the Indian legends at their tongue tips. But as yet she was ignorant in this matter, and therefore fell considerably in the children's estimation. Alary was somewhat hurt by noticing, perhaps for the first time, Sagastao and Minnehaha whispering confidentially to each other. The children conversed with Mary only in her own language, which at that time they perhaps understood better than they did English. Now, much to Mary's annoyance, their confidential whisperings were carried on in English. Being sensitive and quick-tempered, when she saw this sudden break in their affections toward her she was inclined to resent it, and asked the reason why she was not allowed to know what they were talking about.

Blunt little Sagastao spoke up at once:

"Minnehaha and I have talked it over, and have decided that unless you tell us better stories, and ones which you know all about, we're going to run away to the wigwam of Souwanas."

This was humiliating and distressing news. Mary fancied she had told them a good story, and that with a few others like it she could satisfy their curiosity and keep them at home until the brief summer would have passed. Not so, however, thought the children. They saw their advantage and were resolved to keep it, and when their lessons were over and they were left entirely in the charge of Mary they taxed the little woman in a way that obliged her to exercise all her gifts as a story-teller, and she was far from being a poor one.

One day she took them out in a graceful birch canoe among the picturesque islands. They landed on one of these islands, and spent some time in exploring its beauties and resting where grew a profusion of the fragrant Indian grass. They were for a time much interested in the various wild birds that then were so numerous and fearless. Beautiful gulls of different varieties were there nesting, and by following Mary's directions the children were delighted to find that they could approach very near to the nests of some of them without disturbing the mother bird while her mate, in fearless confidence, stood on guard beside her.

"Now, Mary, hurrah for a story!" cried the children, as they sat at lunch.

While Mary was wondering what she would tell them, Minnehaha, with all the restless, inquisitive spirit of childhood, noticing the ceaseless rustling movements of the leaves in the stately northern poplar while the leaves of all the other trees were so still, said:

"Why is it, Mary, that even while the leaves on the other trees are so quiet those almost round ones are ever stirring?"

Mary knew the Indian legend, and at once proceeded to narrate it.

"It is believed by our people," said Mary, "that there are other persons just as clever as Nanahboozhoo, and as able to do wonderful things, but they are very seldom heard of. Some of them were the children of Wakonda, the powerful spirit who dwelt in the region of Spirit Lake, where they say it is always sunshine. Many strange things have been told about them, but everybody says they are kind-hearted, and never did anything to injure any of our people unless it was well deserved. The story is that long ago one of these sons of Wakonda, whose name was Wakontas, could not find a wife to suit him in his own beautiful country, and so he came to the regions where the Indians dwelt.

"For a long time he wandered throughout great regions of country before he found anyone who interested him. However, in his journeyings Wakontas went into the wigwam of some Indians where there were two lovely maidens, so very beautiful that he fell in love with both of them. He was in the disguise of a very fine-looking young hunter. So clever was he in the use of his bow and arrow that at the end of every hunting excursion he returned laden with the richest spoils of the chase. He fell more and more in love with the two girls, and knowing, of course, that he could only get one of them he found a great difficulty in making his choice. He had already gone to the girl's father, and after finding out from him the price demanded for his daughter, without mentioning which one, very quickly by his magic powers he obtained the heavy price and laid it at the father's feet. Both of the girls seemed equally pleased with him, and each one secretly hoped that she might be the object of his choice. Still he hesitated, and although he tried many experiments yet they so nearly equaled each other in cleverness and beauty that he was still undecided. However, there was a great difference in their dispositions. While one was proud and jealous, and had a very bitter tongue, the other was just the opposite; while one was very selfish, the other was generous and kind-hearted. But Wakontas was not able to find this out at first, and after he had considered various plans he decided that he would put on one of his many disguises and thus try them.

"So he started off as though going on a hunting expedition, but soon after he was out of sight he quickly assumed the form of a poor and aged Indian, and came to the home of these two beautiful sisters, and asked for assistance. Wakontas chose a time when he knew the rest of the family were away from the wigwam, in order that he might see how the two sisters would act toward him.

"When he walked into the wigwam, for nobody ever knocks at an Indian tent, the maidens were a little startled at thus suddenly seeing this rough-looking old beggar-man in their midst. The selfish, proud girl, whose name was Misticoosis, at once began assailing him, and cried, 'Auwasta kena!' (Get out; go away, you!)

"In vain he pleaded that he was aged and hungry. She would not listen to him.

"Omemee, the other young Indian maiden, who had not said a word, but had been pitying him from the first moment she saw how feeble and sad he looked, now interfered, and remonstrated with her sister, whose tongue kept up a constant stream of abuse. Taking the old man to her side of the wigwam she seated him on a rug of deerskins and then built up before him a bright fire. Then she quickly brought in venison, cooked it nicely, and gave him the broth for drink and the meat for food. He thanked her gratefully, but she checked his words and said that her greatest joy was in making others happy. Not satisfied with what she had done, and noticing that his shoes were old and worn, she took out of her beaded workbag a pair of splendidly worked moccasins, and put them on his feet.

"All this time, while this good-hearted, generous Omemee was treating the poor old man so kindly, the proud, selfish Misticoosis was talking as hard and as fast as she could against such deeds of kindness to all old people. In her opinion, when they had got so old and helpless as that old fellow was, they ought to be killed by their relatives.

"The old man again expressed his thanks to the kind sister, and then went his way.

"Soon the girls began to think of arraying themselves for the return of their friend and lover. The proud, selfish Misticoosis spent all the time in fixing herself up in the most elaborate manner. She had lately become quite jealous of her sister, and she was resolved to so outshine her in appearance that the handsome young hunter would surely prefer her. But Omemee (a name which means a dove) thought to herself:

"'My father and mother and the rest of the family will soon be returning to the wigwam, tired and hungry, and the best thing I can do will be to have a good dinner ready for them all.' So, only taking time to comb and brush her luxuriant hair and make herself neat and tidy for her work, she set about cooking the meal. She skillfully prepared venison and bear's meat, and the finest of fish.

"Hardly had she finished her work and seen everything nicely cooked before she heard the happy shoutings of her younger brothers, and the sweet birdcalls of her little sisters.

"As Omemee and her sister Misticoosis hurried out to greet them they were surprised to see the handsome stranger gliding along in his beautiful canoe alongside of the larger one of the family. Of course, the sight of their lover excited the two girls. Misticoosis, who had spent all the hours in arraying herself in her finery and adornment, boldly thrust herself to the front, and crowded out the modest Omemee, who was flushed by the busy work of cooking the dinner, and was wisely dressed in a costume which harmonized with her face and with the work in which she had been engaged so industriously.

"The instant the handsome young Indian landed--fancy the amazement of the two girls to notice that he had on his feet the same beautiful moccasins that, not many hours before, Omemee had given to the aged feeble man! Before anyone could utter a word he came striding up to the girls, and said:

"'As an old, weary man, I came to your wigwam a few hours ago. Misticoosis gave me nothing but abuse, yet my only crime was that I was old. Her tongue went on and on without stopping, and all of her words were words of abuse for the old man and anger that he should have been left to live so long. But Omemee, kind-hearted Omemee, pitied the poor old man. She made him sit down on a couch of deerskins, that he might rest his tired limbs. She built a fire and warmed him. She took of the best of the venison, and made him food and drink, and then ere he left she put on his feet the most beautiful of her moccasins. All her gifts to the unknown old man were the best she had.

"'See the beautiful moccasins, the gift of Omemee!

"'I was that old man--I am now the lover long seeking a bride. I have made my choice. Two beautiful maidens for a time divided my heart. There is no division now. By testing them I have found out that only one is lovely within.

"'That no man may have to put up through life with the unceasing clatter of the tongue of Misticoosis, she will be from this time the unbeautiful aspen tree, while her tongue shall be the leaves that will never again be still even in the gentlest breeze. The leaves of other trees shall rest at times, but the aspen leaves, now the tongue of Misticoosis, shall ever be restless and unquiet.'

"And even while he was speaking, Misticoosis, who was amazed and ashamed at the words he spoke, became rooted to the ground, and gradually turned into an aspen tree.

"Then, turning from her to the maiden of his choice, he exclaimed:

"'But Omemee, the loving, the tender, the kind-hearted, thou art my heart's choice!'

"Saying this, the handsome hunter opened his arms, and Omemee sprang toward him. For a moment he held her in his arms; then he said:

"'I am Wakontas, and to the beautiful home of Wakontas thou shalt be taken.'

"Then there was a wonderful transformation; as quickly as a butterfly bursts from its chrysalis, so suddenly was Omemee transformed into a beautiful dove and the hunter as quickly assumed the same lovely form. Together they arose into the air, and flew away to the unknown but beautiful home of Wakontas, in the land of perpetual sunshine."

CHAPTER V.

The Startling Placard--What Happened to the Little Runaways--The Rescue--Mary Tells Them the Legend of the Swallows--How Some Cruel Men were Punished who Teased an Orphan Boy.

When Mary entered the children's bedroom one bright, pleasant morning she was amazed at finding both of the beds empty and a piece of foolscap paper pinned to the dressing table. The writing on it was beyond her power to read. She remembered now that the children had begged her not to come very early in the morning to wake them up, and as their requests were as a law she had lingered as long as she dared, and indeed had only gone to call them when her mistress had asked the reason for their nonappearance. Not until she had shown the paper, with its inscription, to the kitchen maid, who could read English, did its full meaning burst upon her. Of course, she was very much troubled, and yet such was her loyalty to the children that she hesitated about letting the parents know what had occurred. She was fully aware that she could not long keep the startling news from them, and yet she was still resolved that never should any information be imparted by her that might bring down upon them any punishment, no matter how much deserved.

It was a long, rough trail through the primitive forest to the wigwam of Souwanas. How long the children had been away she could not tell. Mary, with Indian shrewdness, had felt their beds, and had found them both quite cold, so she knew the little mischiefs had been off at least an hour. She interrogated not only the maid in the kitchen but also Kennedy, the man of all work, outside. Neither of them had seen or heard anything of the children, and as they did not share Mary's ideas the escapade of the children was soon known.

The parents were naturally alarmed when they heard the news. At once the father, accompanied by Kennedy and the dogs, Jack and Cuffy, started off on the trail of the runaways. The intelligent dogs, having been shown a couple of garments recently worn by the missing boy and girl and being told to find them, at once took up the trail in the direction of the wigwam of Souwanas, running with such rapidity that if they had not been restrained by the voice of their master they would very quickly have left him and his Indian attendant far behind.

At length, with a sudden start, both dogs, growling ominously, dashed off ahead, utterly regardless of all efforts made by their master to restrain them. This suspicious conduct on the part of the dogs of course alarmed the father and his Indian companion, and as rapidly as the rough trail would allow they hurried on in the direction taken by the dogs. Soon their ears were greeted by a chorus of loud and angry yelping. Fear gave speed to both the men, and soon they dashed out from the forest into the opening of an Indian's clearing. Here was a sight that filled them with alarm, and almost terror. Standing on a pile of logs were little Sagastao and Minnehaha. Sagastao erect and fearless, with a club about as large as an ordinary cane, while behind him, leaning against a high fallen log, was Minnehaha. Surrounding them were several fierce, wolfish Indian dogs, among whom Jack and Cuffy, wild and furious, were now making dire havoc. One after another, wounded and limping, the curs skulked away as the two men rushed up to the children.

"Ha! ha! hurrah for our Jack and Cuffy; aren't they the boss dogs!" shouted the fearless little runaways, and now that the victory was won they nimbly sprang down from their high retreat and, apparently without the slightest fear, congratulated both their father and the Indian on the superiority of their own dogs.

Trembling with anxiety, the anxious father, thankful at the narrow escape of his children, as he clasped them in his arms could not but be amazed at the indifference of the little ones to the great danger from which they had just escaped. After petting Jack and Cuffy for their great bravery and courage the return journey was begun, much to the regret of the children, who pleaded hard to be allowed to resume their trip to the wigwam of Souwanas to hear the stories of Nanahboozhoo.

The father was perfectly amazed at this request, and of course it was sternly refused. He had started off in pursuit of the runaways with a resolve to punish them for this serious breach of home discipline, but his alarm at their danger and his thankfulness for their escape had so stirred him that he could not punish them nor even chide them at the time. All he could do was to bring them safely home again and, as usual in such emergencies, turn them over to the tender mercies of their mother.

Sturdily the children marched on ahead for a while, then Kennedy, the Indian, took Minnehaha in his arms. He had not carried her many hundred yards before the weary little one fell fast asleep, softly muttering as she slipped off into the land of dreams, "Wanted to hear about Nanahboozhoo."

Great was the excitement at home when the party returned. Sagastao rushed into the arms of his mother, and without the slightest idea of having done anything wrong began most dramatically to describe how "our Jack and Cuffy thrashed those naughty Eskimo dogs" that chased Minnehaha and him upon that great pile of logs. Mary in the meantime had taken from Kennedy's arms the still sleeping Minnehaha, and almost smothered her with kisses as she bore her away to bed.

There was great perplexity on the part of the parents to know just what to do to impress upon the little ones that they had been very naughty in thus running away, for it was very evident from the utterances of both that they had not considered the matter in that light. Now, in view of the weariness of Minnehaha, it was decided to leave the matter of discipline in abeyance until a little of the excitement had passed away.

In the meantime Sagastao was ready to talk with everybody about the whole affair. It seems that he and Minnehaha had decided that Mary was "no good" in telling stories. He said her stories neither frightened them nor made them cry, but Souwanas was the boss man to tell Nanahboozhoo stories. He said they got up before anybody was stirring, that morning, and dressed themselves so quietly that nobody heard them. They remembered the trail along which Souwanas and Jakoos had carried them. After they had walked for some time they came to where there was a larger trail, and they turned into it, and came upon a lot of dogs that had been chasing some rabbits. Soon the rabbits got away from the dogs, when they reached those trees that had been chopped down. Minnehaha was the first to notice that the dogs had turned back, and were coming after them, and she shouted:

"'O, look! those dogs think we are rabbits, and they are coming for us!'"

"When I saw they really were coming," said Sagastao, "Minnehaha and I jumped up on the logs, and we climbed up as high as we could, and I took up a stick, and then I stood up with Minnehaha behind me, and I shook the stick at them, and--and I shouted:

"'A wus, atimuk!'" (Get away, you dogs!)

"They came so near on the logs that I hit one or two of them, while all of the others on the ground kept barking at us. But I kept shouting back at them, 'A wus, atimuk!' My! it was great fun. Then all at once we heard Jack and Cuffy, and, I tell you! soon there was more fun, when our big dogs sprang at them. Every time an Eskimo was tackled by Jack or Cuffy he went down, and was soon howling from the way in which he was shaken. And they had nearly thrashed the whole of them when papa and Kennedy came rushing up. I wished they had been there sooner, to have seen all the fun."

Thus the lad's tongue rattled on, while it was evident he was utterly unconscious of the danger they had been in.

After some deliberation it was decided that, in view of this runaway being the first offense of the kind, the punishment should be confinement to their own room the next day, until six o'clock in the evening, on a diet of bread and water. At this Mary was simply furious. She well knew, however, that it was necessary for her to control herself in her master's and mistress's presence. She managed to hold her tongue, but her flashing eyes and an occasional mutter, which would come out as she went about her usual duties, showed the smoldering fire that was burning inside. The children had been duly lectured for their breach of discipline and then, that evening, consigned to their room for their imprisonment which was to last until the next evening. That night Mary took up her mattress and blankets and went and slept on the floor between the two beds of the children, and in spite of orders, so the maid said, she secretly carried up a goodly sized bundle from the kitchen.

The day was one of unusual quietness, as the lively pair, who generally kept the house full of music, were now supposed to be away in humiliation and disgrace. All regretted that the punishment had to be inflicted and the children made to realize their naughtiness in thus running away, and all were looking forward to the hour of six o'clock with pleasant anticipation. When it arrived word was sent to the children that their hours of imprisonment were over, and that they were to present themselves in the library. Quick and prompt was the response, and noisily and hurriedly the two darlings came rushing down the stairs, followed by Mary. They were arrayed in their most beautiful apparel, and were evidently prepared by their nurse to go with her for a walk.

The father, feeling that it was necessary, began to make a few remarks expressive of regret that he had thus been obliged to punish them, when he was interrupted by little Sagastao with the honest and candid remark, spoken in a way which, while perfectly fearless, was yet devoid of all rudeness or impertinence:

"O, father dear, you needn't feel badly about us at all, as Mary has been with us all day and has told us lovely stories."

"And Mary brought us taffy candy," broke in darling Minnehaha, with equal candor; "and some currant cakes and other nice things, so we got on very well after all."

These candid utterances on the part of the two children not only amazed but amused the parents, and were another revelation of Mary's wonderful love for the children and her defiance of disciplinary measures which she thought might cause the slightest pain or sorrow. And here she stood in the open door, and as soon as their father's words and their own rather startling "confessions" were ended she called them to her and away they went for a long walk along the beautiful shore of the lake, leaving their parents to conjecture whether the punishment that had been inflicted would produce any very salutary results.

When the children were gathered that evening in the study with their parents little Sagastao said:

"Papa, Minnehaha and I have been talking it all over with Mary and she has shown us that it was naughty on our parts to run away as we did; and we are sorry that we did anything that caused you and mamma sorrow and anxiety about us, and so, ... Well, we know you will forgive us." And as the four little arms went twining around the parents' necks there was joy and gladness all round, and it was evident that there was no danger of the escapade being repeated.

The following are a couple of the legends that Mary told them while they were prisoners in their own room that day.

THE LEGEND OF THE SWALLOWS.

"Long ago," said Mary, "there were some Indian families who lived on the top of a very high hill, like a mountain. They had quite a number of small children, and I am sorry to say they were very naughty and would often disobey their parents. One of their bad deeds was to run away, and thus make the father and mother very unhappy until they returned. Their parents were very much afraid that some of the Windegoos or wild animals would catch them when they thus ran away by themselves, with no strong man to guard them.

"So the parents tried to make their homes as nice as possible for them. They made all sorts of toys for them and gave them nice little bows and arrows, and other things, that ought to have amused them and kept them happy at home. All the efforts of their parents, however, were of no use. They soon were tired of their home amusements, and when their parents' backs were turned they would run away.

"At length their conduct became so bad, and the parents found themselves so powerless to prevent it, that they decided to appeal to the Indian Council for assistance. For a time the stern commands of the Chief were listened to and obeyed. Then they neglected his words, and about as frequently as ever they were found playing truant from their homes and parents.

"At length, on one occasion when they had all run away and had been off for several days and could not be found, their fathers and mothers called upon Wakonda to look for them and to send them home. Wakonda was very angry when he heard about these naughty children running away so much, and so he set off in a hurry to find them. After a long search he discovered them on the bank of a muddy river making mud huts and mud animals. He was so angry at them that he at once turned them into swallows, and said, 'From this time forward you will ever be wanderers and your homes will always be made of mud,' and so it has been."

"I say, Mary, did you remember that yarn because Minnehaha and I ran away?" said Sagastao.

"Well, we were not making mud huts," said Minnehaha.

Mary was not to be caught, however, even if she did love them so much, and she did not answer Sagastao's question, although in her heart she was not sorry if he saw something in the legend that would deter him from again running away.

HOW SOME CRUEL MEN WERE PUNISHED WHO TEASED AN ORPHAN BOY.

"There was once an old grandmother who was left alone with only an orphan grandson. All of her other relatives were dead. This boy was a very industrious little fellow, and did all that he could to help his grandmother. They both had to work very hard to have sufficient to keep them from starving. Together they would go out in their canoe and catch fish. They also set many snares in the forest to catch rabbits, partridges, and other small game.

"Because they were so poor the clothing of this orphan boy was made partly of rabbitskins and partly of the skins of birds. When he was not busy helping his grandmother he, like other little boys, was pleased to go out and play with the other children of the village. Some of the men of the village were very fond of teasing him, and some were even cruel to him, because of the poor clothing he had to wear. Often the poor boy would return to the wigwam of his grandmother crying and weeping because the men of the village had not only teased him on account of his poor clothing but had almost torn his coat into pieces. His grandmother entreated the men to stop teasing the poor boy, who could not help his poverty. She would patiently mend his poor torn clothes and try to cheer him up with the hope that soon these foolish, cruel men would see how wrong it was to treat him thus.

"But they only seemed to get worse instead of better, and so the grandmother got very angry at last and determined to have it stopped.

"So she went off to Wakonda and told him all about it. Wakonda was very busy just then, but he gave her some of his magical powers and told her what to do when she reached her home.

"When she arrived there she found her grandson almost naked from the abuse of the cruel men, who, finding that she was absent, had been more cruel than ever to him. She then informed him that she was able now to put a stop to all their cruel actions. So she told him to dive into a pool of water that was near at hand. He did as she had commanded, and there he found an underground channel that led out into the great lake.

"When he came up to the top of the water in the lake he found himself transformed into a beautiful seal. He at once begun playing about in the waves as seals are often seen doing.

"It was not long before he was seen by the people of the village, and, of course, the men were very anxious to secure this valuable seal. Canoes were quickly launched and away the men paddled with their spears to try and capture it. But the boy, now transformed into the seal, quickly swam away from them, as instructed by his grandmother, and so kept them busy paddling on and on farther from the shore. When they seemed almost discouraged the seal would suddenly dive down, and then reappear in the water just behind them. Then, before the men could turn around and spear him, he as suddenly dived under the water again. The pursuit was so exciting that these cruel men did not notice how far out from land they had now come. They did, however, after a time see their danger, for suddenly a fierce gale sprang up, and the waves rose in such fury that they upset the canoes and all of the wicked men were drowned. When the old grandmother saw this she once more exerted the magical powers with which she had been intrusted by Wakonda, and calling to her grandson to return home he instantly complied with her request. He speedily swam back to her, and she at once transformed him into his human form.

"Thus freed from his tormentors, he very rapidly grew up to manhood and became a great hunter, and was kind to his grandmother as long as she lived."

CHAPTER VI.

Souwanas Tells of the Origin and Queer Doings of Nanahboozhoo--How He Lost His Brother Nahpootee, the Wolf--Why the Kingfisher Wears a White Collar.

W ho was this Nanahboozhoo that we are hearing so much about?"
Thus was the old story-teller addressed by Sagastao, who always was anxious to learn about those who interested him.
The old man began in this way:
"When the great mountains are wrapped in the clouds we do not see them very well. So it is with Nanahboozhoo. The long years that have passed since he lived have, like the fogs and mists, made it less easy to say exactly who he really was, but I will try to tell you. Nanahboozhoo was not from one tribe only, but from all the Indians. Hence it is that his very name is so different.

"The Ojibway call him Mishawabus--Great Rabbit; the Menomini call him Manabush. He had other names also. One tribe called him Jouskeha, another Messou, another Manabozho, and another Hiawatha. His father was Mudjekeewis, the West Wind. There was an old woman named Nokomis, the granddaughter of the moon, who had a daughter whose name was Wenonah. She was the mother of twin boys, but at their birth she died and so did one of the boys. Nokomis wrapped the living child in soft dry grass, laid it on the ground at one end of her wigwam, and placed over it a great wooden bowl to protect it from harm. Then in her grief she took up the body of Wenonah, her daughter, and buried it, with the dead child, at some distance from her wigwam. When she returned from thus laying away her dead she sat down in her wigwam, and for four days mourned her loss. At the end of that time she heard a slight noise in her wigwam, which she soon found came from that wooden bowl. Then as the bowl moved she suddenly remembered the living child, which she had forgotten in her great grief at the loss of its mother. When she removed the bowl from its place, instead of there being the baby boy she had placed there she beheld a little white rabbit, and on taking it up she said, 'O my dear little rabbit, my Manabush!' Nokomis took great care of it and it grew very rapidly.

"One day, when Manabush was quite large, it sat up on its haunches and hopped slowly across the floor of the wigwam, and caused the earth to tremble.

"When the bad Windegoos, or evil spirits who dwell underground, felt the earth to thus tremble they said, 'What is the matter? What has happened? A great Munedoo (spirit) is born somewhere.' And at once they began to devise means by which they might kill Manabush, or Nanahboozhoo, as he was now called, when they should find him.

"But Nanahboozhoo did not long continue to look like a rabbit. As he was superior to other people he could change himself to any form he liked. He was most frequently seen as a fine strong young Indian hunter. He called the people his uncles. When he grew up he said to his grandmother, the old Nokomis, that the time had come when he should prepare himself to go and help his uncles, the people, to better their condition. This he was able to do, seeing he was more than human, for his father was the West Wind and his mother a great-granddaughter of the moon. Sometimes he was the beautiful white rabbit; then he would be a wolf or a wolverine; then he would be a lovely bird. He could even change himself to look like a dry old stump or a beautiful tree. Sometimes he would be like a little half-frozen rabbit; then he would be a mighty magician, and often a little snake. He was just as changeable in his disposition as in his outward appearance. Sometimes he was doing the best things imaginable for his uncles, the Indian people, and at other times he was full of mischief and trickery. But on the whole he was a friend, and although quick-tempered and fiery yet he did lots of fine things for the people, for he was really one of the best of the Munedoos of the early times.

"When the time came for him to leave his grandmother's wigwam he built one for himself, and then he asked Nokomis to prepare for him the sacred magical musical sticks which she alone could make. His grandmother made him four sticks, and with these he used to beat time when singing his queer songs. Some of them were very queer, and ended up with 'He! he! ho! ho! ha! ha! hi! hi!' Others were in reference to some special benefits he would confer on his uncles. In one of them, referring to his going to steal the fire for them, he sings:

"'Help to my uncles I'm bringing, Their sorrows I'll change into singing. From their enemies the fire I'll steal, That its warmth the children may feel.

"'Disguised will be Nanahboozhoo, That his work may the better be done; But his jolly deeds ever will tell who Has been sporting around in his fun.'

"At first he was a jolly fellow, full of fun, and did lots of good things for his uncles. He showed them the plants and roots good for food, and taught them the arts of surgery and medicine, but as the years went by he did some things that caused him to be feared very much. His uncles always went to him when they got into trouble, but whether he would help them or not depended much on the humor he was in when they came.

"After he had lived for years in the first wigwam which he had built, and taught the people of the earth many things, his father, the West Wind, held a council with the North Wind and the South Wind and the East Wind, and as Nanahboozhoo was never married, and was living such a lonely life, they determined to restore to life, and give to reside with him, his twin brother who had died at his birth. The name of this brother was Nahpootee, which means the Skillful Hunter. Nanahboozhoo was very fond of him, and took great care of him. He grew very rapidly, and he and Nanahboozhoo were very great friends. Like Nanahboozhoo, Nahpootee could disguise himself in any form he chose. One favorite form he often assumed was that of a wolf, as he was often away on hunting excursions. The evil spirits, or Windegoos, who dwell under the land and sea, had never been able to do much harm to Nanahboozhoo, he was too clever for them; and although they often tried he generally worsted them. Now they were doubly angry when they heard that Nahpootee had been restored to life and was living with him. Nanahboozhoo warned his brother of their enmity, and of the necessity of being on his guard against them.

"These brothers moved far away and built their wigwam in a lonely country on the shore of a great lake which is now called Mirror Lake, because of its beautiful reflections. Here, as he was a hunter, Nahpootee was kept busy supplying the wigwam with food. Once, while he was away hunting, Nanahboozhoo discovered that some of the evil Munedoos dwelt in the bottom of the very lake on the shores of which they had built their wigwam. So he warned his brother, Nahpootee, never to cross that lake, but always to go around on the shore, and for some time he remembered this warning and was not attacked. But one cold winter day, when he had been out for a long time hunting, he found himself exactly on the opposite side of the lake from the wigwam. The ice seemed strong, and as the distance was shorter he decided that, rather than walk around on the shore, he would cross on the ice. When about half-way across the lake the ice broke, he was seized by the evil Munedoos and drowned.

"When Nahpootee failed to return to the wigwam Nanahboozhoo was filled with alarm and at once began searching everywhere for his loved, lost brother. One day when he was walking under some trees at the lake he beheld, high up among the branches, Ookiskimunisew, the kingfisher.

"'What are you doing there?' asked Nanahboozhoo.

"'The bad Munedoos have killed Nahpootee,' Ookiskimunisew replied, 'and soon they are going to throw his body up on the shore and I am going to feast on it!'

"This answer made Nanahboozhoo very angry, but he concealed his feelings.

"'Come down here, handsome bird,' he said, 'and I'll give you this collar to hang on your neck.'

"The kingfisher suspected that the speaker was Nanahboozhoo, the brother of Nahpootee, and he was afraid to descend.

"'Come down, and have no fear,' said Nanahboozhoo, in a friendly tone. 'I only want to give you this beautiful necklace to wear, with the white shell hanging from it.'

"On hearing this the kingfisher came down, but suspecting that Nanahboozhoo would be up to some of his tricks he kept a sharp watch on him. Nanahboozhoo placed the necklace about the neck of the bird so that the beautiful white shell should be over the breast. Then he pretended to tie the ends behind, but just as he had made a half knot in the cord, and was going to tighten it and strangle the bird, the latter was too quick for him and suddenly slipped away and escaped. He kept the necklace, however, and the white spot may be seen on the breast of the kingfisher to this day.

"Soon after this the shade or ghost of Nahpootee appeared to Nanahboozhoo and told him that, as his death was the result of his own carelessness, in not keeping on the land, he would not be restored to live here, but was even now on his way to the Happy Hunting Grounds, in the Land of the Setting Sun, beyond the Great Mountains.

"Nanahboozhoo was deeply moved by the loss of his brother, who had been such a pleasant companion to him. So great was his grief that at times the earth trembled and the evil spirits dwelling under the land or water were much terrified, for they knew they would be terribly punished by Nanahboozhoo if he should ever get them in his power. But it was a long time before he had an opportunity to get his revenge on them for the death of his brother. How he did it I will tell you at some future time."

CHAPTER VII.

The Legend of the Bad Boy--How He was Carried Away by Annungitee, and How He was Rescued by His Mother.

Tell us, Mary, a story about the boys of the old times among the Indians," said Sagastao.

"About bad boys," said Minnehaha with a mischievous look in her eyes; "for this morning brother and papa had to have a 'settlement,' and it might do Sagastao good to hear about other bad boys and what was done with them."

These words of Minnehaha made Mary very angry. She thought more of Sagastao than she did of any other member of the family, and nothing threw her into a rage quicker than for anyone to cross him or even to question the wisdom of anything he said. Now, indignant that his father had been obliged to call him into his study for some misdemeanor, Mary was greatly annoyed to hear these words.

"O, pshaw, Sakehow," said Sagastao; "do not be so touchy. I deserved the talking to that papa gave me. It was wrong of me to whack that Indian boy with my bat as I did, and I ought to have been punished; so if you have any jolly good stories about bad Indian boys, and how they were punished, why, let us have one."

This confession of her favorite, who, after his temper cooled, was always quick to admit that he had been in the wrong, quite pacified Mary, and she settled down on the wolfskin rug with the children and began her story.

"Long ago all the Indians believed in Windegoos and other spirits that were more or less friendly to good people. Some were man-eaters and, of course, were always to be feared. Some Indians were in such fear of these cannibals that they would never leave the wigwam after dark for fear of being gobbled up by some of the monsters that might be skulking about.

"There was one great creature called Annungitee, or Two Faced. He had a great habit of looking out for bad boys, very bad boys. It was said that he could not see really good boys; that they were like glass, and he could not see them. But when a boy became very bad he was then so black that he was easily seen, and Annungitee could espy him a long way off and was very likely to come after him.

"Fortunately Annungitee always made a noise when he was passing along. This was a good thing for bad boys, for it gave them time to scurry into the wigwams, out of his way. He was so big that when he set one of his feet down on the ground there would be sounds like the ringing of bells and the hooting of owls. When he put the other foot down the sound was like the roaring of buffalo bulls when they are going to fight each other. Even when he tried to move softly there would be sounds like birds and beasts crying out. All the Indians who had heard this great terrible fellow were afraid of him, and yet no two were able to give the same description of him. But they did agree on one thing, and that was that when he caught a very wicked man, which he did sometimes, or very bad boys, which he often did, he just threw him into one of his big ears and held him there. Indeed, it was believed that he could hold three big men or six bad boys in one of his ears at the same time. Nobody knew where he lived, as no one had been found brave enough to follow and see, and no daring hunter had ever found his abode in any of his hunting expeditions.

"Now a certain Indian man and his wife who lived in a wigwam quite apart from other families had one boy. He was their only child. He had been a very bad, cruel, unkind boy. His father had to work hard as a hunter to obtain sufficient game to keep them from starving. His mother cut the wood, carried up the water from the distant river, dressed the skins of the animals that were shot by her husband, and did all the work of the wigwam. The boy would not lift a finger to help in any way. One day the mother, who was quite sick, asked him to go for some water. He refused, and was very saucy to her. Then she asked him if he would please bring in some wood for her, as she felt cold. No, he would not do anything of the kind. She then became quite angry with him, and said:

"'If you do not be a better boy I will put you out of the wigwam, and Annungitee will toss you into his ear.'

"All the same, she did not really believe he would, as she had not heard of Annungitee or any other kind of ghost being around for a long, long time. She only said what she did to frighten the bad boy into obedience. Indeed she had often said to him, when she was angry with him, 'I do hope a ghost will catch you.' But the more she talked to him the worse he became. So one day when he had been very lazy and very rude to her she sprang up and, seizing him by the arm, undertook to put him out of the wigwam. He became much frightened at this and began to cry. But she, knowing that he deserved to be punished, pushed him out and securely fastened the doorway, calling out:

"'May Annungitee catch you!'

"She did not really mean it, of course. No mother could wish her boy to have such a terrible misfortune. The frightened boy then began running round and round the wigwam, trying to find some place where he could get in, but he could find no opening. After a while his crying and his efforts to get into the wigwam ceased, and all became still and silent. His mother listened attentively, and every moment expected to hear his voice again, but there was no sound except something like the sound of the singing of birds and the rattling of small bells dying away in the distance. At this she became very much frightened and began to cry, and to call for her boy. She threw open the door flap and began to search all around her wigwam for her son. But all in vain! He was nowhere to be found.

"When the father came home from his hunting she told him of the sudden disappearance of their boy, and he, too, was very much alarmed. They set out and visited the lodges of all the people around. But no one had seen or heard anything of the missing boy. They returned to their own silent wigwam very sorrowful, and for days they mourned over the loss of their son. One night, as the mother was weeping on account of her great loss, she heard some one crying out to her:

"'Hi! Hi!' and at the same time she heard the sounds of bells ringing and owls hooting. This happened several nights, and then one night there was a voice saying:

"'You said, "Ghost, take that boy." Hi! Hi!'

"Next morning the wife told her husband what she had heard during the previous night, and she added:

"'I believe the ghost Annungitee has taken our boy.'

"Her husband was very angry when he heard this, and said:

"'Yes, a ghost has taken our boy. You gave him to him, and he has taken you at your word. So why should you complain? It serves you right.'

"At this the mother lifted up her voice and cried out so loud that it could be heard a great distance.

"'Husband,' she said, 'I deserve what you have said, but I am going to try and get back our boy, and so to-night I will hide in the pile of wood that is outside the wigwam, and if the ghost comes along again, as he has been coming, I will catch him by the leg, and you must rush out and try to rescue our son.'

"So that night she hid herself in the wood pile, and, sure enough, after a while she heard the sound of bells ringing and animals softly crying out, and then a loud 'Hi! Hi!' after which all was still.

"Then, as she cautiously looked out from her hiding place, there before her was a great creature standing beside the wigwam. He was so tall that his head was higher than the smoke hole at the top, and he was peeping down into the wigwam. But, big as he was, she had a mother's loving heart after all, and as she thought of her boy fastened up there in one of his big ears she was determined to rescue him if possible. So she cautiously moved along until she was able to seize one of his legs, which she did with all her strength, and at the same instant she shouted for her husband to come and help. Out he rushed, and between them they tumbled the tall ghost over and, sure enough, in one of his big ears they found their little boy.

"Poor little fellow. He was half-starved, and so thin and weak that he could hardly stand. But they helped him into the wigwam and gave him some soup, made out of some birds that his father had killed that day.

"The tall ghost was so frightened by the sudden way in which he had been seized that as soon as he could get up he hurried away, and was never seen in that part of the country again. Some tribes say he went South, and there, when he was stealing children and carrying them off in his ears, he was caught by the angry parents and burned to death on a big wood pile."

"Did the little boy get better?" asked Minnehaha.

"O yes, he did, after a while; but he was a long time in getting over the fright he had had. It did him good, however, for after that he was never rude and saucy to his mother and did all he could to help her."

"Did it do the mother any good?" asked Sagastao, who had not been altogether satisfied with her treatment of the boy.

"Yes, indeed," said Mary; "for after that terrible fright she was never known to shout out at her boy such words as, 'I hope the ghost will catch you,' or any other of the unpleasant ones which she sometimes had used when she was angry with him."

"Thank you, Sakehow," said both the children. "A pretty good story, that."

Then what a jolly romp they had with Jack and Cuffy! The two splendid dogs were the children's special protectors and companions.

CHAPTER VIII.

Happy Christmas Holidays--Indians Made Glad with Presents--Souwanas Tells How Nanahboozhoo Stole the Fire from the Old Magician and Gave It to the Indians.

The Christmas holidays were times of innocent festivities and gladness among the Indians and their white friends, both at the mission and at the trading post.

The gifts which it was possible to give to the Indians were not of very great value, but they were articles much needed and were always prized by the recipients even if they were never very profuse in their words of thanks. Minnehaha and Sagastao were wild with delight at these times, and were eager to be the almoners of the mission, and carry the gifts to the Indians whom they loved so well. The fact that the temperature of those bright, cold Northern winters kept steadily many degrees below zero did not chill their ardor nor lessen their enthusiasm. Their dog trains were in almost constant demand, for they kept flying over the various icy trails until in the different wigwams all had been remembered with some useful gift.

Faithful Mary had made for them the warmest of fur and blanket suits. Dressed in these, and tucked in among the robes in the cariole by their careful driver, they sped along the trails. They made the woods echo with their merry shouts and laughter--unless it was so bitterly cold that they had to be completely covered up. It is not to be wondered at that there were times when, on reaching some distant wigwam, there were little hard, white spots on their cheeks or noses which told the watchful Indians that the Frost King had been at work and that speedily those frostbites must be removed. Little cared they for the momentary pain that ensued, when the frozen parts were being thawed out. They were out for a good time, and they had too much grit and courage to let such trifles as a few frostbites disturb their happiness. The bright fires burning in the center of the wigwams, or in the fireplaces at the end or side of the little Indian houses, were of course always welcome after a long run in the bitter cold.

"Tell us, Souwanas," said Sagastao one very cold day, as they were gathered around his wigwam fire, "how it was that Nanahboozhoo stole the fire from those who were guarding it and gave it to the Indians."

"It must not be too long a story," said Minnehaha, "as we have yet to go to the wigwam of Kinnesasis, Little Fish, with his presents, and it would be too bad to be late when they know we are coming."

So Souwanas pledged himself to make the story as short as he could without spoiling it, and then, after a few more whiffs from his beloved calumet, he began:

"It was long ago, when there were fewer people in the forests and on the prairies than now. They did not have as many comforts as they have now, and one of the rarest things among them was fire. Sometimes when the lightning's flash set a tree on fire they would have it for a little while, but they did not seem to be able to keep it going, and they were often very cold and generally had to eat their food without cooking it.

"Nanahboozhoo was then still living with his grandmother, Nokomis, and was sorry to see that she often suffered from the cold and that the food was miserable because it was not cooked. So he set his wits to work and decided that something must be done. As he should now have to deal with the Muche Munedoos, evil spirits, he had to be very careful. He put himself in various disguises and at length he heard all about how the coyote had stolen some of the fire from the watchers in the underground world, who possess enormous quantities of it. It frightened him a little when he heard that there was so much fire in the world under us, but he was not apt to be afraid very long and so as he went on searching, and on the sly listening to the talks of windegoos and others, he found that the fire for which he had been so long searching was in the possession of a fierce old medicine warrior who guarded it with the greatest care. Those who had employed the coyote to get it had intrusted its keeping to him. In those days they had an idea that fire was such a dangerous thing that it would be almost certain destruction to the race if it was given to all. This old warrior had his two daughters, who were great, fierce women, to assist him in guarding the fire.

"Several attempts had been made to steal the fire ere Nanahboozhoo resolved to see what he could do. All of these other efforts had failed, and the parties who tried them were killed. Nokomis heard of these unsuccessful attempts and tried to dissuade her grandson, Nanahboozhoo, from such a dangerous enterprise.

"Nanahboozhoo, however, was a very skillful fellow, and although this was one of his first great undertakings, for it was long ago, he was not to be stopped by her fears, and so away he went. As the ice was not yet on the waters he took his birch canoe and paddled eastward as far as he could. Then he hid his canoe where he could easily find it on his return.

"The next thing he did was to transform himself into a rabbit, and in that shape he hurried on until he saw in the distance the sacred wigwam where dwelt the old guardian of the fire and his two daughters, who were famous for their height and their strength. To excite the pity of these daughters Nanahboozhoo jumped into some water, and then crawling out, wet and cold, he slowly approached the wigwam. Here the two daughters found him, and he looked so miserable that they took pity on him and at once carried him into the wigwam and set him down near the sacred fire, that he might soon get warm and dry."

"How very kind that was of the old man's daughters," said Minnehaha.

"I don't know about that," said the more matter-of-fact Sagastao; "folks sometimes get into trouble by taking up everything that comes along. Remember that old rascal that humbugged father."

But Souwanas, remembering his promise, adroitly shunted off the youngsters and resumed his story.

"The two girls, after seeing how contented and happy the rabbit seemed to be as it warmed itself by the fire, again returned to their duties in different parts of the large wigwam. The rabbit soon after hopped a little nearer to the fire, that he might be able to seize hold of a burning stick or brand, but as he moved the ground shook and trembled under him so that it awoke the old man, who had fallen into a heavy sleep. Thus disturbed, he called out to his daughters in alarm:

"'My daughters, what was it that caused the ground to tremble?'

"The girls replied that they did not know. They had done nothing beyond their usual work except to bring in to warm a poor little shivering half-frozen rabbit that they had found outside. At first the old man was a little suspicious and, rolling over, he took a good look at Nanahboozhoo. But he had made himself into such a poor little wretched half-drowned rabbit that the old man's suspicions were completely dispelled, and he turned over again and went to sleep.

"Nanahboozhoo was pleased to hear the old man snoring again, and he only waited now until the two girls should both be busy in the wigwam on the opposite side from the door; then he suddenly changed himself into a fleet young Indian runner, and quickly seizing hold of a burning stick he dashed out of the wigwam and away he rushed toward the place where he had left his canoe.

"Of course there was instant pursuit. The two daughters, although they were magicians, like their father, well knew that they would be punished by the superior evil spirits if they allowed any of the sacred fire to be stolen, and they were furious at the cunning and deceitful Nanahboozhoo, whom they now recognized, for playing such a trick upon them. Shouting to their father, to arouse him, they immediately ran after the retreating Nanahboozhoo, who with the burning brand in his hand was speeding rapidly over the trail. But, fleet as he was, he soon discovered that the two girls, by their magic, were rapidly gaining upon him. They were the fleetest of runners, even if they were girls, and it was for that reason that they and their father were intrusted with the sacred fire. Great honors were to be theirs if they guarded it to the satisfaction of those who had intrusted it to them, while, on the other hand, great would be their disgrace if they failed in their duty.

"When they found that they were gaining on Nanahboozhoo, and were likely to regain possession of the firebrand, with shouts and threats they declared that severe indeed would be his punishment, when he fell into their hands, for his abuse of their kindness and his trickery.

"Nanahboozhoo felt that he was indeed in a tight place. He did not, however, intend to be overtaken, and he sped on, if possible faster than ever, until there was only a large dried-up, barren meadow between him and the spot where he had tied his canoe on the shore of the lake. The girls were only a few hundred yards behind him, and he resolved to fight them with this sacred fire. So, as he rapidly continued his flight, he plunged the now blazing firebrand into the dry grass, here and there, on each side of the trail. The wind was in his face, and it carried back the fierce blaze and dense black smoke and not only quickly hid him from the sight of his pursuers but also made it very dangerous for them to follow him.

"Nanahboozhoo thus succeeded in reaching his canoe, and fixing the burning brand in one end of the boat he was soon rapidly paddling over the waters toward his distant home. The flying sparks of the torch burnt him badly in several places, but he did not much mind this, and he dared not stop to dress his wounds for fear that his pursuers would yet overtake him.

"Fortunately he succeeded in reaching his distant home. There at the shore to welcome his return was Nokomis, who had been full of anxiety about him. She carefully dressed his burnt face and hands and gladly received the gift of the fire, which has been such a blessing to the Indians ever since.

"At first there was a good deal of trouble among the Indians to keep the fire burning. Sometimes the watchers appointed to look after it, especially in the summer months, would forget to add fresh fuel, or would go to sleep and neglect it. Then they would have to send off to some perhaps distant wigwam, where the people had been more careful, and secure some live coals from them.

"Nanahboozhoo was troubled about this. He feared that if it were allowed to die out at the same time in all of the wigwams he might not be so successful again if he had to try to get a fresh supply from the fierce old man and his now wrathful daughters. So he went out into the woods and at length a good spirit came to him in a dream and told him of various ways in which the fire could be obtained. He showed him how it could be made, by rapid friction, with dry sticks. Another way he revealed to him was by the striking together of a flint stone and a piece of iron; sparks of fire could thus be produced which, caught in punk, would soon become a blaze. So now the Indians do not have to cover up the fires as they were formerly obliged to do; thanks to Nanahboozhoo's dreams, they can make it fresh whenever they want it."

"Hurrah for Nanahboozhoo for his good work this time!" said Sagastao.

"Well, I think he was a mean fellow, to so fool those two nice girls who took him in and warmed him when he was a poor little wet shivering rabbit!" said Minnehaha.

"Took him in?" the lad retorted. "Well, I guess it was well he was able to take them in as he did, by setting fire to that old grass in the meadow, for if he had not done so they would soon have had his scalp."

But here Minnehaha appealed to Souwanas, and said:

"I have been wondering how it was the old man and his daughters got the fire in the first place from out of the underground. Will you not tell us that story some time?"

The old man looked grave and was silent for a minute or two, then he replied:

"I think you had better ask Kinnesasis. He knows the story better than I do, for in his youth he traveled far West, into the land of the high mountains, where the legend is that the fire was stolen out of the center of the earth."

"All right. Thank you, Souwanas. We are going to take Kinnesasis some presents, and while there we will ask him for the story."

Here an Indian lad rushed into the wigwam with the word that Kennedy was coming with their cariole. The children were well wrapped up, and soon with their usual happy, "Wat cheer! Wat cheer!" they were speeding homeward.

CHAPTER IX.

Kinnesasis--How the Coyote Obtained the Fire from the Interior of the Earth.

A great time the children had in the wigwam of Kinnesasis. He was such a jolly little old Indian, and he was specially happy to-day when the children opened out the gifts and presented them. He was more than delighted with a suit of black clothes sent him from a distance by friends who had heard about him and his needs. He quickly put on the whole suit, which fitted him very nicely, and then much amused the children by saying:

"I am sure the man who made these clothes is in heaven, or, if not yet dead, he will go to heaven when he dies."

"Why, Kinnesasis, it is the kind friends who sent you these clothes you ought to thank, and not make such a fuss over the man who made them; he was paid for making them," said Sagastao. But Kinnesasis could only think of the man who made the suit of which he was so proud.

Kinnesasis's old wife was, if possible, still more delighted with her presents than the old man with his. She and Minnehaha were always the best of friends, and now as the child handed her gift after gift of warm clothing and food her joy knew no bounds, and, old as she was, when some warm shoes were given her, she sprang up and began singing an Indian song, while with all the agility of a young maiden she spun around the wigwam in rhythmic measure to her words, which, roughly translated, are as follows:

"The Good Spirit has pity on me,   Though for days I had little to eat,   I was wretched and sad in my heart,   I was cold, O so cold! in my feet.

"But now I have plenty of meat,   Clothes for my body, shoes for my feet,   I'll not grumble, nor sorrow, but praise   The Good Spirit the rest of my days."

"Well done!" shouted the children when the old woman stopped. They were greatly delighted with her performance. Kinnesasis, however, who, as well as his wife, was now a church member, professed to be much shocked at seeing her thus dancing, as though in the wild excitement of the Ghost Dance. But both Sagastao and Minnehaha stood up for the old wife. They said the words she sang were good enough for the church, any day, and they were sure nobody could find fault with her thus showing how glad and thankful she was.

And nobody ever did find fault and soon was the affair almost forgotten, for now the merry jingling of more dog bells was heard, and who should come into the wigwam of Kinnesasis but the parents of Sagastao and Minnehaha!

Cordially were they greeted. At first it was difficult for them to recognize the staid little gentleman in his full suit of broadcloth as the lively but generally ill-clothed Kinnesasis. The visitors--who quickly saw and were delighted with the transformation--greeted him as though he were some distinguished stranger. This vastly amused the children. Screaming with laughter at Kinnesasis's pretense of keeping up the farce, they shouted out, "Why, this is only our dear old Kinnesasis. He is no great stranger. It is only Kinnesasis with his new clothes."

"Well," then was asked, "who is that charming old lady over there with such a fine shawl and brilliant handkerchief on, and such fancy new shoes on her feet? Surely she is a stranger."

"No! No!" the children again shouted. "Why, that is Kinnesasis's wife, with her new presents on! My! doesn't she look nice!"

Here the little ones seized hold of the happy old Indian woman and made her get up and show herself off in her new apparel, of which she was just as proud as Kinnesasis.

"And she gave us such a jolly dance in them, papa! Wouldn't you like to see her do it again?" cried Minnehaha.

But here Kinnesasis, pretending to be shocked beyond measure, in a most diplomatic manner directed the attention of the parents to some other matter, and so the mischievous child did not succeed in making a church scandal by inducing one of the flock to dance before the missionary.

"Tell us, Kinnesasis," said Sagastao, "how it was that that old man and his daughters first obtained the fire which Nanahboozhoo so cleverly stole from them and gave to the Indians long ago."

At first Kinnesasis hesitated about telling the old legend, saying that he did not think the father and mother of the children would care for such stories.

"Don't they, though!" cried the children. "You don't know them very well, then, if you don't know that they like stories just about as well as we do."

And with this they at once appealed to the parents, who of course sided with them and expressed their desire to listen to this story that the children had told them they were to hear from dear old Kinnesasis.

Throwing some more logs on the fire, around which the white visitors with the Indians gathered, Kinnesasis began:

"It was long ago, when I was a young lad, that I heard the story from the old story-tellers of our people. I had traveled with my father for many days far toward the setting sun. We reached the land of the great mountains, and there, with our people of those regions, we spent some moons. It was while we were among them that I heard from the ancient story-teller the legend of how the fire was stolen from the center of the earth, where it was kept hidden away from the human family.

"That there was such a thing as fire was well known. It had been seen bursting out of the tops of distant mountains, and there had been times in great thunder-storms, when the lightning had set fire to dead trees--and indeed in this latter way the Indians had become acquainted with its value to the human race. But they had not taken care to keep it burning, and no one had been appointed to specially look after it.

"The reason why fire had not been from the first given to men was because when the race was created the fire was not much needed. The earth was then much warmer than it is now. There was no snow or ice ever seen except on the tops of the very highest mountains. Great animals now all dead, and others that could only live in the hottest countries, lived all over these great lands. Then there was abundance of fruit and nuts and roots that were all very good for food. Then some great disaster happened to the world and soon it began to grow colder and many animals, and even families, perished. Snow and ice appeared where they were never seen before. There was great suffering from the cold. The hunters began to kill the animals for food. They were now not satisfied with the fruit and roots, they wanted something better.

"So the fire was much needed. But where it was, or how to get it, was the question. Fortunately an old dreamer dreamed a dream about it. As the council assembled to hear his dream he told them that the fire was preserved in the heart of the earth by a magician called Sistinakoo, and that it was kept very carefully surrounded by four walls, one within the other, in each of which was a single door. At the first door a great snake kept guard. At the second door a mountain lion or panther was the guardian. A grizzly bear guarded the third door, and at the fourth and last door Sistinakoo himself kept watchful care over the precious fire that smoldered on a stone altar just inside this last wall.

"When the council heard all this they were almost discouraged. They thought it would be impossible for anyone to get by all of these guards and steal the fire.

"They first asked the fox to try, but he only reached the first door when the great snake nearly made a meal of him. Thoroughly frightened, he rushed back to the top of the earth and told of his narrow escape.

"For a time nothing more was done to try and get the fire. The people continued to suffer, for the earth kept getting colder and colder and ice and snow were now to be found in lands that had previously been comfortably warm. So the council was called again, and the question again raised as to what could be done.

"It happened that there came to the council a very old man who remembered a tradition, handed down from his forefathers, which said that part of the earth beneath us was hollow, and that some of the animals, even the great buffaloes, had dwelt in those underground regions before they came to dwell on the surface of the earth. He said that the coyote, the prairie wolf, was the last one to leave, and that he was sure that he still remembered the route to the very spot where Sistinakoo, the head chief of the regions, guarded the fire so jealously."

"Why should they so guard the fire, and be so careful about letting people have it, when we know how good it is?" asked Minnehaha.

"Because," replied Kinnesasis, "there was a tradition that at some time or other the fire should get the mastery over men, and the whole world be burned by it, and they thought that they would carefully guard it from getting scattered about by careless people who might set the world on fire."

"Well, go on, Kinnesasis, and tell us the rest of the story," said the impatient

Sagastao.

"So when the Indian council heard this story they sent for the king of the coyotes and told him of their wish that he should return to that underworld and bring up the fire for their use.

"To their surprise and great delight the coyote said he would go, and he immediately began his preparations for the journey. So greatly had the cold increased that he found the dark mouth of the entrance under the mountains almost surrounded by snow and ice. After traveling for some time in the darkness he reached the outer wall, where he waited, a little distance from the door, until the snake was taking his usual sleep. Then he quickly stepped past him. Knowing the habits of the other animals, he waited until they were asleep and then he noiselessly passed them all. Even Sistinakoo himself was sound asleep. So the coyote crept silently up to the fire and lighted the large brand or torch that was securely fastened to his tail. The instant it began to blaze up, as the coyote rushed out through the first door, Sistinakoo shouted, 'Who is there? Some one has been here and has stolen the fire!'

"He at once began to make a great row and loudly called to the different keepers to close the doors in the walls. But the coyote was too quick for them all, and ere the sleepers were wide enough awake to do anything he had passed through all the doors and was far on his way to the top of the ground. The fire was gladly received by the people, but after some time, when some big prairies and forests had been burned up by it, the men got fearful that the world might be destroyed and so they intrusted it to the care of the old magician and his two daughters, with orders to be very careful to whom they gave any. It was from them Nanahboozhoo stole it, to scatter it once more freely among the people as we now have it.

"But the tradition was still believed in the days of my grandfather that, good as the fire was to warm us, and cook our food, it would yet become our master, and do the world much harm."

Kinnesasis was thanked by all for his recital of this suggestive legend, especially by his older listeners, who saw much in it that was in harmony with the earlier beliefs of other nationalities. By this time, however, the dogs in their trains were impatiently barking, and longing to get back home for their suppers. So, after farewell greetings to Kinnesasis and his wife, one cariole after another was loaded, and away the happy ones sped over the icy expanse of the frozen lake.

CHAPTER X.

The Christmas Packet--The Distribution of Gifts--A Visit by Dog Train, at Fifty-five Below Zero--Souwanas Tells How the Indians first Learned to Make Maple Sugar.

How great the excitement was which attended the arrival of the Christmas packet can hardly be realized by persons who have never been exposed to the privations of a land which the mail reaches every six months, and where they wait half a year for the daily paper. After this long waiting it is no wonder that a great shout was raised when far away in the distance the long-expected, heavily-loaded dog-trains were seen that for several hundred miles had carried the precious messages of love and the tokens of good will from dear ones far away.

This year an extra train well loaded with much-needed supplies for the mission was among the arrivals. Its coming was hailed with special delight by the children; for even in that Northland Santa Claus was not unexpected, and it was surmised by some of the wee ones that possibly some of his gifts would arrive about that time.

And they were not disappointed, for loved ones far away in more favored lands had remembered these little ones in their Northern home, where the Frost King reigns, and many and varied were the gifts which they now received.

"I am going to take Souwanas some of my candies," said Sagastao.

"And I am going to give him a nice red silk handkerchief," said Minnehaha.

The children had by this time pretty well learned his weakness for these things, and it was a pleasure now for them to think that they had it in their power to make him happy.

The next morning was, as usual, bright and cloudless, but it was bitterly cold. The mercury was frozen in one thermometer, and in the other one the spirit indicated fifty-five below zero. Yet so impatient were these spirited children to be off with their gifts to Souwanas, and with something also for each member of the family, that their pleadings prevailed. A cariole with plenty of fur robes was soon at the door, and with old Kennedy as their driver they were soon speeding away behind a train of dogs.

Indians are naturally alert and watchful, and so the merry jingle of the silvery bells was heard while the cariole was still at some distance on the trail. Cordially were they welcomed, and strong arms speedily carried them into the cosy wigwam where, in the center, burned a great fire of dry spruce and birch wood.

As the cold was so intense, and the children had permission to remain for two hours, it was decided that Kennedy should return home at once with the dogs, as it would have been cruel to have kept them out in the cold so long.

The heavy wraps were soon removed and the children were comfortably seated on the fur rugs provided for them. Then they very proudly opened their parcels and distributed the contents--their own gifts as well as those which had been sent to Souwanas and his family from the mission. Minnehaha reserved her special gift for the last. When all of her others had been bestowed she unfolded the beautiful red silk handkerchief and, going over to Souwanas, she did her best to tie it nicely around his neck.

The old man, genuine Indian that he was, was much moved by her winsome ways and handsome gift.

He said but little, but there was a soft, kindly look in his eyes that showed his gratitude more than any words could have done. It meant a good deal more than perhaps he would like to admit and those who saw it were thankful that they had observed it, knowing that it meant so much. Sagastao, who had already given him several presents, had held on to his box of candies. He had learned that for such things the old man could be coaxed to do almost anything, and now he held them out, and said:

"Now, Souwanas, as all the presents have been passed around, I have got some fine sweeties for you, but we must have a first-class Nanahboozhoo story for them."

"O yes!" said Minnehaha. "And as it is to be for sweeties let us have a nice sweet story of Nanahboozhoo this time."

"A sweet story you want? Well, before I begin let us fix up the fire and all get comfortably seated around it."

Then, as they usually did, the two white children cuddled as close to the inimitable story-teller as they could. Little cared they for the cold without or even for the occasional puffs of smoke which seemed at times to prefer to enter the eyes of the listeners rather than to go out at the orifice at the top of the wigwam.

"A sweet story," musingly said the old man, "in this land of fish, and bears, and wolves, and wildcats, and wolverines!" Then he paused long enough to fill his mouth again with the candies which he enjoyed so much.

"A sweet story. Then it must be of a land, south of this, where for some years I dwelt, many, many moons ago. A land where the Se-se-pask-wut-a-tik (sugar maple tree) grows and flourishes in all its beauty.

"There, in those wigwams, long ago lived the people whom we call the Hurons, the Dakotahs and the Ojibways. These Ojibways are cousins of my own people, the Saulteaux. Well, the story I want to tell you had its beginning long, long ago. One day there came a great embassage of Indians from the far South with words of peace and good will. They said that in their country they had no cold weather, and very seldom saw any snow. They said that the trees were different, and that many things grew there that they did not see in our Northern country. They brought with them many presents and were kindly received by our people, and then, after some weeks of feasting and speech-making, they returned home laden with the best gifts our tribes could bestow.

"Among the presents which these Southern Indians brought was a large quantity of sugar. This was the first time it was ever seen among the Indians of the North. It was very much prized, and was very carefully divided among the people so that each one had a small quantity. It did not last very long, for everybody was fond of it. When it was all gone the people were sorry, and the question was asked, 'Why cannot we send a company of our own people and get more of it?'

"This suggestion met with the favor of the tribes, and a large party of the best runners was selected, and being well supplied with rich presents and pipes of peace they started off to find the Southland and to obtain abundance of the sugar. Some weeks passed by before word was heard from them, and the news was very bad. Fierce wars had broken out among the tribes that lived between ours and those who dwelt in that far South. Our Indians had to fight for their lives. Many of them were killed, others were badly wounded, and of the large company that started out not more than half ever returned to their homes. The expedition was a complete failure.

"Still there was the memory of the sugar among them, and it happened that one day in the council somebody said:

"'Why not send to Nanahboozhoo?'

"Good!" shouted Minnehaha; "that is just what I thought they would do."

"Well, hold on," said her more matter-of-fact brother; "just as like as not Nanahboozhoo would give them salt instead of sugar, if he were in one of his tantrums."

Souwanas was not displeased at this interruption on the part of the children, and gladly availed himself of the opportunity thus offered to once more help himself to the sweets.

Earnestly appealing to Souwanas, Minnehaha, who always looked on the bright side of things, and who had a quick intuition quite beyond her years, said:

"It could not be a sweet story if Nanahboozhoo gave them salt instead of sugar; could it, Souwanas?"

The old man, as soon as his mouth was sufficiently emptied to resume his story, amused by the earnestness with which the child appealed to him, replied with the words, "Tapwa, tapwa!" (Verily, verily!)

Sagastao, however, unwilling to give in, retorted, "O 'tapwa, tapwa' doesn't mean anything, anyway."

Souwanas only laughed at this criticism, and proceeded with his story.

"So it was decided to send a deputation to Nanahboozhoo to tell him of the wish of the tribes to have Se-se-pask-wut (sugar), as had the tribes of the Southland.

"The deputation who started off to find Nanahboozhoo had a great deal of difficulty in finding him. It seems that a great strife had arisen between Nanahboozhoo and some of the underground Muche Munedoos--bad spirits, sometimes called the Ana-mak-quin--who had determined to kill Nokomis, the grandmother of Nanahboozhoo, because of their spiteful hatred of Nanahboozhoo, whom they knew they could not kill because he had supernatural powers.

"Nanahboozhoo had, as usual, been playing some of his pranks on them, and that was why they were determined to kill Nokomis."

"What were some of the tricks that Nanahboozhoo had been up to this time?" asked Sagastao.

"It would take me too long to tell you now," replied Souwanas.

"Nanahboozhoo dearly loved his grandmother, although he was often giving her great frights, just as other grandsons sometimes do. So when he heard of what the Muche Munedoos were threatening he took up his grandmother on his strong back and carried her far away and made for her a tent of maples in a great forest among the mountains. The only access to it was across a single log at a dizzy height over a wild rushing river.

"It was now in the fall of the year, and the leaves of these trees were all crimson and yellow, so brilliant that when seen from a long distance they looked like a great fire. Thus it happened that when the bad spirits following after Nanahboozhoo and Nokomis saw the brilliant colors through the haze of that Indian Summer day they thought the whole country was on fire, and they turned back and troubled them no more. Nanahboozhoo was pleased that the beautiful maple trees had been of so much assistance to him. He decided to dwell among them for some time, so he prepared a very comfortable wigwam for himself and his grandmother.

"It was in the wigwam among the maples that the deputation found Nanahboozhoo. He received them kindly, and listened to their story and their request.

"At first Nanahboozhoo was perplexed. He was such a great traveler that he had often been down in the great Southland, and well knew how the sugar was there made. He had seen the fields of sugar cane, and knew the whole process by which the juice was squeezed out and then boiled down into sugar. He also knew that it required a lot of hard work before the sugar was made.

"When Nokomis heard the request of the deputation to her grandson she was very much interested--for had not Nanahboozhoo several times, when returning from those trips to the South, brought back to her some of the sugar?--and she had liked it very much; and so now she added her pleadings to theirs that he would in some way grant them their request.

"Of course Nanahboozhoo could not refuse now, so he told them that, as the beautiful maple trees had been so good to him and Nokomis, from this time forward they should, like the sugar cane of the South, yield the sweet sap that when boiled down would make the sugar they liked so much.

"He told them, however, that it was not for the lazy ones to have, but only for those who were industrious and would carry out his commands. Then Nanahboozhoo described to them the whole process of sugar making. He told them that only in the spring of the year would the sweet sap flow. Then they were to have ready their tapping gouges, their spiles and buckets. Great fireplaces were to be built and here, as fast as the sap was gathered from the trees, it was to be boiled down in their little kettles into the nice molasses; and then a little more, so that when it cooled it would harden into sugar.

"'Now,' added Nanahboozhoo, 'go back to your people and tell them that it depends on their industry between now and the spring who shall have the most of the sugar you love so well.' Then he skillfully modeled out a stone tapping gouge of the shape required to make the incision in the tree from which the sap would flow. With his knife he made a sample spile of cedar, the thin end of which was to be driven into the hole made by the gouge and along which the sap would flow. Then he told them to make plenty of buckets of birch bark, and thus be ready when the time came to secure an abundant supply of sap. Thus the art of making maple sugar first came to be known. Nanahboozhoo gave it to the Indians long ago. Then when the palefaces came they followed the same process. That is the way Nanahboozhoo showed us how to get the maple sugar."

But here the sound of the barking of the dogs, and the sweet tones of the silvery bells on the collars of the dogs that had come for the children, told that the two hours had passed away.

"Thank you ever so much," said the grateful Minnehaha, as she rose to have loving hands carefully wrap her up for the return ride, "for that sweet, sweet story. It was so good of Nanahboozhoo to tell them about the sap in the maple trees, even if it is only there in the spring time."

"I think old Nokomis deserves a good deal of the credit," said Sagastao. "It seems to me that Nanahboozhoo would not have done it if she had not made him."

"Well, Nanahboozhoo did it, anyway, and so we and the Indians have our maple sugar and molasses, and I am glad. And so, hurrah for Nanahboozhoo!" Thus replied Minnehaha.

Here Souwanas lifted the well-wrapped-up child, and carried her out to the cariole, where she and her brother were speedily covered and tucked in among the warm robes.

"Marche! Marche!" was shouted to the dogs by the driver, and away they sped over the icy trail with such speed that it was not long ere they were again safe and happy in their own cozy home.

CHAPTER XI.

Mary Relates the Legend of the Origin of Disease--The Queer Councils
Held by the Animals Against Their Common Enemy, Man.

Mary, how is it that I get sick sometimes," said Sagastao the following summer, "and have to take medicine that I dislike? Why can't we always be well?"

For the last week or ten days Mary had been most devoted and faithful in watchful care over her restless charge, who had been very sick but was now rapidly recovering.

"As soon as you are a little stronger I will tell you the legends of sickness and medicine, as handed down by our Indian forefathers," said Mary, "but now you must only rest, and eat, and sleep."

"Well, Sakehow" (beloved), his pet name for his faithful nurse, "I will try and mind you; don't forget."

The next week was one of rapid recovery, and very proud, indeed, was Mary when she led forth the two children, in the bright sunshine of a delightful summer day, to a cozy resting place among the rocks where the waves of Lake Winnipeg rippled on the sandy beach at their feet.

Minnehaha was eager for a story about the sweet birdies or the brilliant flowers, but the young invalid had his way this time, and Mary proceeded to tell the story of the Indians' idea as to the origin of sickness and disease.

"Long, long ago," said Mary, "all the animals and birds on this earth lived in peace and harmony with the human family. Then there was food for all in abundance without any shedding of blood. Even the wild animals, that now live by killing and devouring each other, found plenty of food in the fruits and vegetables that then were so abundant.

"Men and women also lived on similar things, and were contented and happy. But as the years went on the people became so numerous, and their settlements spread over so much of the earth, that many of the poor animals began to be cramped for room.

"Even this could have been borne, but by and by men began to make bows and arrows, spears and knives, and other weapons, and began to use them on the defenseless animals. Then soon they began to eat the flesh of the animals, and presently they found that they preferred the meat thus obtained to the fruits and vegetables of the earth.

"Formerly they had made their garments out of the fiber of the trees and plants, which the women carefully prepared and wove; but after a while they discovered that the skins of the buffalo and deer and other animals, when well prepared, made better and more durable garments and wigwams than the materials they had previously used. As time went on the destruction of the larger animals increased, and men became so much more cruel than formerly that even the frogs and worms, that in the earlier days were never harmed, were now destroyed without mercy, or by sheer carelessness or contempt. Thus the animals came to be in such a sad plight that it was resolved by them to call great councils of their members together to consult upon what could be done for their common safety.

"The bears were the first to assemble. They gathered together on the peak of a great smoky mountain, which the white men now call Cathedral mountain, and the great white bear from the Northland was appointed chairman."

"Well, that was funny," said Minnehaha. "Just fancy a big white bear sitting up in a chair! Why, he would need a whole sofa to hold him."

"Don't be silly, child," said the patronizing brother. "It was a bears' council and, of course, the chairs used were bears' and not men's."

When Mary was appealed to to settle the question she could only say, "As the council was held on the top of a mountain perhaps the bears sat on the rocks. But never mind; let me go on with the story.

"After the white bear had made his speech he took his seat and said he was now ready to hear the statements of the different bears who had assembled to lodge their complaints against the way in which men killed their relatives, devoured their flesh for food, and made garments and robes out of their skins.

"Nearly every kind of bear had grievous statements to make, and so blood-curdling were some of their recitals that it was decided to begin war at once against the human race.

"Then the question was asked, 'What weapons shall we use against them?' After some discussion it was decided to use bows and arrows, the favorite weapons of their enemies.

"'And what are they made of?' was the next question.

"This was soon answered by a bear who had been caught when young and kept captive for a couple of years in the wigwam of one of their enemies. He had often seen the process of making bows, and he was now able to tell all about it, and even to do the work himself. It was not long before the first bow, with some arrows, was manufactured, and there was great excitement when the first trial of it was made. A large strong bear was selected to shoot the first arrow. To their great disappointment the trial was not a success, for it was found that when the bear let the arrow fly, after drawing back the bow, his long claws caught in the string and spoiled the shot. Other bears tried, but they all had long claws, and they all failed. Then some one suggested that this difficulty could be overcome by their cutting off their long claws. But here the chairman, the white bear, interposed, saying that it was very necessary that they should have their long claws in order to climb trees, or up steep rocky places. 'It is better,' said he, 'for us to trust to our claws and teeth than to man's weapons, which certainly were not designed for us.'

"The bears remained in council until they got very hungry, but think as much as they might they could not devise any satisfactory plan, for they are stupid animals after all, and they dispersed to their different homes no better able to fight the human race than before.

"Then the deer next held a council. Representatives of all the different kinds of deer, from the great elk and moose down to the smallest species in existence, assembled in a beautiful forest glade. The moose was selected as chief. After a long discussion it was resolved that in revenge for man's tyranny they would inflict rheumatism, lumbago, and similar diseases upon every hunter who should kill one of their number unless he took great care to ask pardon for the offense. That is the reason why so many hunters say, just before they shoot, 'I beg your pardon, Mr.

Deer, but shoot you I must, for I want your flesh for food.' They know that if they do this they are safe.

"The Cree legend is that it is the bear that has to be propitiated by gentlemanly expressions when he is being approached to be killed. I well remember being with a couple of hunters closely following up a bear, and just before they fired they kept saying, 'Excuse us for shooting you, Brother Bear, but we must do it. We want your warm fur robe, our families want your meat, our girls want your grease to put on their heads, so you must excuse us, Brother Bear. Please do, Brother Bear; please do.' Thus they went on at a great rate until he was killed.

"But many forget it, and the spirit of their chief knows it and is angry, and he strikes those hunters, or their relatives, down with rheumatism or some other painful disease.

"Next the fishes and snakes and other reptiles held their council, and they decided that as the human race had now become such enemies to them they would trouble them with 'fearful dreams' of snakes twining about them, and blowing their poisonous breath in their faces, by which they would lose their appetites and die, while others of them would seek opportunity to make the water they drank, or even the air they breathed, unwholesome. The poisonous ones were also directed to use every opportunity to kill with their deadly bites whenever possible.

"The birds also held a council, over which the crow was appointed chairman. The eagle objected, and wanted the place, but he was voted down because there were so few of his kind, and these were only hunted for their feathers to adorn the war bonnets of the great chiefs and warriors. The crow was appointed because he was always with the human race and knew the various schemes and tricks they were inventing to injure the birds and animals of various kinds. After much deliberation the birds decided to give colds, and coughs, and throat diseases, and consumption, to the human race, and to thus lessen their numbers that there might be room for all creatures.

"The insects and smaller animals then held their council, and the grubworm was appointed to preside over the gathering. He was so elated over his election, and that they had arranged a scheme which should be fatal especially to women, that he fell over backward and could not get on his feet again. So from that time the grubworm has only been able to wiggle in that way. There was any amount of talking and buzzing among the crowd. The frog was especially noisy and angry in his remarks.

"'It is high time,' said he, 'that we began to do something against this cruel human race, or we will soon be swept off the earth. See how my back is ugly with lumps and sores because men have so kicked and knocked me about!'

"Others followed in the same strain of indignant protest against man's cruelty. Even the flies and mosquitoes had something to complain of.

"Well, after the buzzing, and the croakings, and the hummings and angry talkings were over, they settled down to business.

"Some were appointed to poison the waters so that malarias and fevers should attack the now hated race. Others, such as the flies and mosquitoes, were to carry in their bites and stings many diseases. Thus it has come to pass that there is more damage done to the hated human beings by these bites and stings than the mere smarting pain caused at the time of the bite. Thus, because the human race changed from being all kindness to the rest of the creatures, both great and small, into being cruel and savage, all these various creatures have combined to bring dreadful diseases among men in revenge for their own wrongs."

"That is too bad," said Minnehaha. "Why could they not have kept on loving each other all the time, instead of things being as they are now?"

Sagastao, who had laughed at the idea of the mosquitoes coming to a council, and of their having anything to complain of, said, "I would like to know what mosquitoes lived on in those good old days you speak about. Now they are after me lively enough." And he slowly lifted up his hand, on the back of which a couple were rapidly filling themselves with his blood.

But Mary, who, Indian like, was wise and observant, only said, "Wait a minute or two and I will show you." Then she quickly hurried back into a swampy place and soon returned with a thick juicy leaf, to the under side of which several mosquitoes were still clinging, with their bodies distended with its juice.

"There," she said, as she carefully held the leaf sideways, "that is what most of the mosquitoes still live on. They attack our race in revenge for our being so cruel as to kill so many of the animals, large and small, but this, as you can easily see, is their natural food."

This appeal to the eye quite silenced the children, who had considered the whole story as only an Indian legend to be amused with.

Mary, who had often been worsted by the sharp criticisms and inquiries with which they were apt to receive her pet Indian legends, was quite delighted at her apparent triumph, so she hastily sprang up, saying:

"It is time we were going home. Some other day I will tell you the story of how the medicines came."

CHAPTER XII.

The Naming of the Baby--A Canoe Trip--The Legend of the Discovery of Medicine--How the Chipmunk Carried the Good News.

There was great excitement among a number of Indian men and women who had gathered on the shore in front of the mission one pleasant summer morning. Grave Indians, with Souwanas in their midst, were calmly discussing some object of interest, while Mary and a party of women, some of whom had their babies with them, were much more noisy, talking rapidly about something which was evidently a matter of exciting interest. Even Sagastao and Minnehaha were rushing in and out of the house and running from one group of Indians to the other, full of eager inquiries and pleasant anticipations. What could it all be about?

Let us ask the children, for such little people often know more than we are likely to give them credit for. Here comes Minnehaha, and we ask her the cause of such an early gathering of the Indians, and the reason why they are so unusually interested in some matter unknown to us.

"Why, don't you know?" the bright little girl promptly replies. "They have come to form a Naming Council, to give my little baby sister an Indian name. You see," she added, "Sagastao and I were born among the Cree Indians, but baby was born here among the Saulteaux. Just think: the first little white baby born among them! And they want to give her a nice Saulteaux name. The reason why they are talking so much now, before they form the council, is that lots of them have pet names they want to give our baby, but of course she can only have one."

"Yes," said Sagastao, "and our old Mary is trying to get the women to oppose the name that Souwanas will offer, just because she is down on him. But I'll bet he will beat her yet."

"You should not say, 'I'll bet.' Mother has often told you that it was very rude," reprovingly said little Minnehaha. "You never learned it from father or mother. You must have picked that up from some rough trader."

"Well, all right, I'll not say it again, but I'll bet--no, I mean--hurrah! for Souwanas and his side, anyway," and off he ran.

"Dear me!" said the little sister. "I do have so much trouble with that boy!"

Soon the council assembled. The men and women arranged themselves in a big circle and spent some time in drinking some strong, well-sweetened tea that had been prepared for them. They had been desirous of having their usual pagan ceremonies, but of course this could not be allowed, so the ceremonies of tea drinking and their usual smoking were substituted. Then the little baby was brought in by her nurse and handed to one of the oldest women. She took the child, and after kissing her and uttering some words of endearment passed her on to the woman on her left. She in her turn kissed her, uttered some kindly words, and passed her on to the next. So baby went from hand to hand until she had made the complete circle of women and men. This was the ceremony of adopting the child into the tribe.

Mary, the nurse of the older children, was excluded from this circle as she was of another tribe. After some more tea had been drunk the child was again sent on her rounds. This time each person, as he or she held the child, pronounced some Indian name that he or she wished the babe to be called. Mary, who had now crowded herself into the circle, persisted in having a voice in the matter. She wanted the child to be called Papewpenases (Laughing Bird), but she was voted down by the crowd, who said:

"No, that is Cree; we must have Saulteaux."

With a certain amount of decorum each name suggested was discussed, only to be rejected.

For a time there was quite a deadlock, as no name could be decided upon.

"Now that you have all spoken," said Souwanas, "and cannot come to any agreement, I, as chief, will make the final decision. This is the first white child born among us, as Sagastao and Minnehaha, whom we all love, were born at Norway House, among the Crees. Most of the names which you have suggested have some reference to birds and their sweet songs. A compound name, which will include these ideas and mine, Souwanas (South Wind), can surely be found."

This suggestion was well received, as Florence was born in the spring of the year, when the birds, returning from the South, filled the air with melody after the long stillness of that almost Arctic winter.

So busy brains and wagging tongues were at work, and the result was the formation of the following expressive name, which was quickly bestowed upon the child. It was first loudly announced by Souwanas himself: Souwanaquenapeke; which in English is, "The Voice of the South Wind Birds."

At once all the Indians took it up and uttered it over and over again, so that it would not be forgotten. Even Sagastao and Minnehaha, who could talk as well in the Indian language as in English, took up the word and shouted out, Souwanaquenapeke, until they had it as thoroughly as their own.

Mary alone was vexed, and so annoyed that she could not conceal her disappointment. This was particularly noticed by Sagastao, and as soon as Minnehaha joined them they slipped quietly away together. Having obtained permission they took a canoe and went for a paddle on the quiet lake. Mary, like all other Indians, was passionately fond of the water, and in spite of her crooked back was a strong and skillful paddler.

The children were placed in the center of the canoe, on a fur rug, while Mary seated herself in the stern and paddled them over the beautiful sunlit waves.

For a time but little was heard, for the children were absorbed in the scenes of rarest beauty or watched some fish, principally the active gold eyes, sporting in the water around them.

After a while the children began to clamor for a story, but Mary would not speak a word. Sagastao suspected the cause of Mary's unusual silence.

"What is the use, sakehou," he protested, "of your being in a pet because baby was not named Papewpenases? The name they gave her pleased everybody else; you must be pleased too."

"If you are cross and won't speak to us we will go and run away to Souwanas; won't we?" said Minnehaha.

This was too much for Mary, and she quickly surrendered and made an excuse about thinking of some beautiful story to tell them when they should land on that little rocky island just ahead of them.

"Very well," said Sagastao, "let us have the one about how medicines were discovered and given to the Indians to cure diseases."

"Just the one I was thinking about," said Mary; "and while we rest on the lovely white sand I will tell you the story."

A few vigorous strokes of the paddle sent the canoe well up on the sandy shore, and soon they all landed. A good romp relieved them of the stiffness caused by the cramped position in the canoe. Then as they cuddled down in the warm sand Mary began her story.

"You remember, little sweethearts, how the animals of various kinds held councils and decided to be revenged on the human family for their cruelty by sending diseases among them. Well, these creatures did as they said they would and the result was that lots of men died, and also the women and children, that did the creatures no harm, were getting different kinds of sicknesses and many of them were dying.

"Were there no diseases among them before these times?" inquired Minnehaha.

"No; not what you might call diseases," replied Mary. "The people lived such simple lives that, with the exception of accident, such as being drowned in great storms or killed by falling trees, or something that way, nearly all the people died of old age."

"Then they had no doctors in those days?" asked Sagastao.

"No; there were no medicine men in those times. Although there were those skillful to set broken limbs or attend to any who happened to be accidentally wounded, but that was nearly all. Then all at once these diseases sent by the angry animals began to appear among them, and, of course, there was much alarm. The people did not know what had brought them, nor how to get rid of them. Many people were sick and numbers of them died.

"You see, the animals held their councils in secret, and away from the presence of men, and so it would never have been known if the ground squirrel, called by some the chipmunk, had not gone and told all about the councils to the men. He had always been friendly to the human race. He had attended a number of the councils and was the only animal that had ventured to say anything in the favor of man. By doing this he so enraged the other animals that some of them fell upon him with great fury, and would have torn him in pieces if he had not been able to escape into his hole in the ground. As it was, they so tore and wounded him with their teeth and claws that the stripes remain in his back to this day.

"Well, when he was healed enough to get around again he visited the abodes of the human race and was very sorry to find that the diseases sent by the other angry animals were causing much suffering and many deaths, so he revealed the whole thing to a number of men and told them to be on their guard. But even this was not sufficient. It was felt that, now that these diseases were spreading among them, they must have some remedies for the cure of them or they would all soon be destroyed.

"While thus wondering what they should do their little friend the ground squirrel came to their help again. He went about among the trees and plants, who were always friendly to man, and he told them of the sad calamities that had come to the human race.

"When the trees and plants heard what had been done by the animals to injure and destroy their friends they speedily held councils among themselves and resolved that they would do all they could to overcome the evil.

"First the great trees held their councils, talked over the matter, and decided what they could do in the way of furnishing remedies to cure these diseases that were doing so much injury. The pine and the spruce and the balsam trees said, 'We will give of our gums and balsams.' The slippery elm said it would give of its bark to make the soothing healing drink. The sassafras said it would give of its roots to make the healthful tea that will bring back health again. The prickly ash and the sumach and others volunteered their help, and spoke of the wonderful healing power there was in them, if rightly used.

"When the plants came to their council the numbers that wanted to help were very great. No one was able to keep a record of them and of the healing powers they professed to have. There was the mandrake, with its May apples, and the wintergreen, with its pretty red berries; the catnip and the bone-set, which are so good for colds; the lobelia, which is such a quick emetic; the spikenard, the peppermint, the snakeroot, sarsaparilla, gentian, wild ginger, raspberry, and scores of others. All cheerfully offered assistance.

"When the ground squirrel, who had for days been attending the council of the trees and plants, had made out his list of what remedies each tree and plant could furnish he was very much delighted, and then, thanking them for their offered assistance, he rapidly returned to the abodes of mankind and informed them of his great success.

"Of course they were very much pleased, and very grateful to the ground squirrel for his kindness and his interest in their happiness. This is the reason why the chipmunk, or ground squirrel, lives near the homes of men. You never see an Indian shoot them or the boys or girls try to snare them. They are always welcome among the trees and the wigwams. The Indians love them because they spoke up for man when the other animals turned against him, and because it was one of their ancestors that made the trees and plants reveal their good medicines for the cure of the sick."

"Now I know why it was, when I was out with the Indian boys, that they never would shoot an arrow at a chipmunk, even when I asked them to," said Sagastao.

"Yes," said Mary, "all of the Indians have heard their fathers tell of the kindness of the old father chipmunk in the days when the animals knew so much and could talk, and so they warn the children against injuring these pretty little creatures."

But it was now time they were returning. The light canoe was once more pushed down into the lake, and soon they were merrily gliding along over the clear, transparent waters to their cozy home.

CHAPTER XIII.

In the Wigwam of Souwanas--How Gray Wolf Persecuted Waubenoo, and How He was Punished by Nanahboozhoo.

We have come to-day for a nice story about Nanahboozhoo," said Minnehaha, as she and Sagastao lifted the deerskin door at the wigwam of Souwanas, and entered with all the assurance of children who knew they were welcome.

"Did he ever do anything to punish bad fellows who were cruel to their wives and children?" asked Sagastao. "Because, if he did, I wish he would come and thrash old Wakoo, that bad fellow who has been thrashing his wife again because he said she did not snare enough rabbits to suit him."

Souwanas, who was one of the kind-hearted Indians, never cruel to any of his family, was much amused at the fire and indignation with which the young lad spoke. So after he had had comfortable seats arranged for the children among the robes and blankets he endeavored to satisfy their demands. "Nanahboozhoo," he said, "did such things long ago, but once, when he was giving a good thrashing to a man who had been very cruel to his wife, the wife, as soon as she was able, sprang up from the place where her husband had knocked her to, seized a paddle and attacked Nanahboozhoo with such fury that he resolved never to interfere again, if he could help it, in a quarrel between man and wife. And," added the old man, with a merry twinkle in his eye, "it is best for everybody, if possible, to keep out of such quarrels."

"Yes, but, mismis" (grandfather, Minnehaha's pet name for Souwanas), "you surely know a nice story in which Nanahboozhoo helped some one without getting into trouble himself."

"Of course I do, my grandchild," said the old man, "and I know you will be pleased with it.

"My story is about a lovely Indian maiden who was bothered by a cruel hunter. He was determined that she should marry him, although she did not like him, and Nanahboozhoo came to her rescue.

"The maiden's name was Waubenoo. She had the misfortune to lose both her father and mother when she was about eighteen years old. There were four children, all much younger than she, left in her sole care. They had no uncles or aunts, or other relatives, near, to take care of them, and so Waubenoo had to hunt and fish to get food for her little brothers and sisters. Fortunately her father had left a number of good traps and nets, and plenty of twine for snares, and so the industrious girl got on fairly well. The great lake near her wigwam was well supplied with fish, and the forests all round had in them many rabbits and partridges and other small game. When great storms arose on the big lake, and Waubenoo could not go out alone in her birch bark canoe to visit her nets, some of the Indians, who were pleased to see how kind and industrious she was, would overhaul her nets and bring in what fish were caught. Thus she toiled on, and with the assistance of these kind Indians she did very nicely. Her little brothers and sisters loved her dearly, and did what they could to help in the simpler and easier part of the work. Every decent person among the Indians was pleased with her industrious habits, and often, in their quiet way, had some cheery words of encouragement for her.

"But there was one exception, and this was a selfish Indian hunter who, seeing what a fine-looking, strong woman she had become, and so clever in her work with both nets and traps, resolved that she should be his wife, to work for him and do his bidding. This man had been married before and, if the reports were true which had been told, it was likely that his wife had died because of his cruelties to her. So he resolved, in his selfishness, to take Waubenoo from caring for her brothers and sisters to be his wife, and to hunt and fish for him, that he might live a life of idleness.

"Her parents being dead this selfish young Indian did not have to go to her father to buy her to be his wife. All he thought he had to do was to go and tell her she had to be his wife and come and do as he commanded her. So harsh and cold were his words, and so very rough and forbidding his looks, that, while Waubenoo was frightened, she was grave and high spirited enough to indignantly refuse his request, and to order him never to trouble her again.

"This, of course, made him very angry. He refused to go, and continued to insist on her going with him.

"Fearing that he might revenge himself upon her by doing her or the children some harm, she told him that it was her duty to stay with the little ones whom the death of the parents had left in her care; that they might perish if she now left them.

"But nothing would turn away his anger, and if it had not happened just then that some friendly Indians came along he would have cruelly beaten her. Before them he durst not strike her, and so, muttering some threats, he sulkily strode away into the forest.

"Poor Waubenoo was now sadly troubled. Lighthearted and free, she had cheerfully worked and toiled for her loved ones, but now here comes this cruel, fierce-looking man, whom she could only look on with fear and dread, and threatens to drag her away from them all. Gray Wolf, for that was his name, had a bad reputation among the Indians. The young men shunned him and the maidens took good care to be out of the way when he was around. That he would persist in his attempts to get Waubenoo all were convinced, but that he should succeed no one desired. Still, while Indian ideas on some of these things are so peculiar that no one seemed disposed to interfere, at the same time some of them were generally on the lookout for her protection. As for brave Waubenoo, while certain that he would still trouble her, she was resolved never to submit to him.

"Thus the weeks rolled on, with Gray Wolf looking for some opportunity to carry her off, and making several attempts to do so, which Waubenoo, ever alert and watchful, succeeded in preventing.

"At length his persistent attempts became so annoying that she was obliged to neglect much of her work in order to keep on her guard. Food was getting scarce because she dared not now go far from her wigwam to hunt for the partridges and rabbits and other small creatures she was so clever in snaring.

"At length she resolved to go to Nanahboozhoo and seek his aid in getting rid of this troublesome fellow. When Nanahboozhoo heard her sad story he became very angry. He was indignant that such a commendable maiden, one who had been so kind to her little brothers and sisters, should be bothered by a big, selfish, lazy fellow who only wanted her because she was so industrious and so clever at her work.

"Nanahboozhoo had heard much about her kindly treatment of the children, and of her skill in providing for their wants, so he lost no time in going back with her to her wigwam. At first the younger children were much afraid of him, as they, like all other Indian children, had heard such wonderful tales about him. But he was in such a jolly good humor that day, and was so delighted with everything he saw about Waubenoo's wigwam and with the proofs of her industry that he soon made friends with all the children. How to go to work to give Gray Wolf such a lesson that he would never trouble them any more he hardly knew at first. However, he had not been there many hours before he had to come to a decision, for one of the little children came rushing into the wigwam with the terrible news that Gray Wolf, carrying a big dog whip and looking very angry, was coming along the trail. Nanahboozhoo only laughed when he heard this, and he very quickly decided what to do. 'Sit down there,' he said to Waubenoo, 'in that dark side of the wigwam, with a blanket over your head, and keep perfectly still until I call you; and you, children, must keep quiet. Do not be frightened or say a word, no matter what happens.'

"Then Nanahboozhoo, who, as you know, could change himself into any form he liked, suddenly transformed himself so as to look exactly like Waubenoo. So perfect was his resemblance to her, even to his dress, that her brothers and sisters could not have detected the disguise. Indeed, the young ones could not help looking over to the spot where the real Waubenoo sat in the gloom with the blanket drawn over her head. But they were Indian children, early trained to be quiet and do as they were told, and so they fully obeyed his commands.

"Of course, when Gray Wolf came into the wigwam he was completely deceived, and now, thinking that he had caught Waubenoo when there were no friendly Indians around, he at once began speaking very fiercely to her:

"'I have asked you for the last time,' he said, 'and now I have come with my dog whip and I intend giving you a good thrashing and then driving you to my wigwam. I intend to call you Atim, my dog, and like a dog I am going to thrash you.'

"He then savagely raised the whip to strike, as he thought Waubenoo, but the blow never reached its victim, or even Nanahboozhoo in his disguise, at whom it was aimed, for Nanahboozhoo was so enraged that anybody in the shape of a man could be so cruel and selfish as to come and threaten a kind young woman like Waubenoo that he suddenly sprang at Gray Wolf, and seizing him by his scalp lock he dragged him out of the wigwam, and then wrenching the heavy whip out of his hand gave him such a terrible beating that he remembered it as long as he lived. Then roughly throwing him to the ground, Nanahboozhoo, still in the disguise of Waubenoo, hurried into the wigwam and said to the real Waubenoo:

"'Now, while he is weak and cowed, go out and talk sternly to him, and tell him that if he ever troubles you again it will be worse for him than this has been.'

"When Waubenoo came out her appearance so terrified Gray Wolf that he tried to get up and skulk away, weak as he was. Waubenoo, glad that her enemy was so conquered that he would not be likely to trouble her much more, did as Nanah-boozhoo requested her.

"Nanahboozhoo was heartily thanked by Waubenoo and the children for thus ridding them of this bad Indian, who had for so long made their lives miserable. Ere he left Nanahboozhoo warned the children to say nothing about his coming, 'for,' said he, 'if Gray Wolf finds out who it was that thrashed him he may yet be troublesome.'

"Well would it have been for all if the children had remembered this advice," added Souwanas.

"O tell us what they did, and what happened," shouted Sagastao.

"Not to-day," said the old man; "it is time you both were back at your lessons, and as I am going that way with some whitefish I will take you with me in my canoe."

"But is that all about the story of Waubenoo and the children?" said Minneha-ha.

"Yes," said Souwanas, "until we come to the next. For a long time after Gray Wolf received the beating he kept away from them, although his heart was full of anger and revenge. Although he was a big fellow he feared to again threaten her who, although she seemed but an ordinary-sized Indian maiden, possessed the strength that had enabled her to give him such a thrashing."

CHAPTER XIV.

The Pathetic Love Story of Waubenoo--The Treachery of Gray Wolf--The Legend of the Whisky Jack.

It came about in this way," said Souwanas, "and it is such a sad story about beautiful Waubenoo."

"Will it make me cry?" said the tender-hearted Minnehaha. "If so, I do not think I want to hear it."

"Stay and hear it, you little pussy," said Sagastao. "I am sure it is not worse than the Babes in the Wood."

"Well, you always cry first, when we read that story together," said Minnehaha.

At this the lad had nothing to say, for in spite of his apparent brusqueness his heart melted more quickly, and his eyes filled easier with tears, at a pathetic story, than did his sister's.

"Well, go ahead, Souwanas," said Sagastao. "We each have a pocket handkerchief, and when they are used up you can lend us a blanket."

At this quaint speech everybody laughed, and then the old man began his second story about Waubenoo. "It all came about because little children have long tongues, and this story should warn little children that, while they have two eyes and two ears, they have but one tongue, and that they should not at any time talk about or repeat half of what they have seen and heard.

"The little brothers and sisters of Waubenoo had been warned that they should say nothing about the visit of Nanahboozhoo to their wigwam. In fact, Nanahboozhoo was such a queer fellow that he did not at any time want people to be gossiping about him, and, if he had done any good deed for anyone, he did not wish them to be ever speaking about it. Then another reason why Nanahboozhoo did not want them to talk about his visit and help was the fear that Gray Wolf, finding out how it was that he had received such a beating, would be more bitter and revengeful against Waubenoo and would again try to get her in his power. The little children were, of course, delighted that their wigwam was no longer visited by Gray Wolf, whose coming had always filled them with terror, while Waubenoo was so pleased at having thus got rid of him that she was happier and brighter than she had been for a long time. It was not long before some of the other Indians noticed the change. They were surprised that Gray Wolf had so suddenly stopped his visits, and that he seemed so dejected and sullen. Naturally their curiosity was excited, and they were anxious to find out what had happened."

"Better to have been minding their own business," broke in young Sagastao, who seemed to see the drift of the story.

"Be quiet, and do not interrupt Souwanas," said Minnehaha, who often felt called upon to restrain her brother's impulsiveness.

"Of course," Souwanas continued, "Gray Wolf had so suffered that he had very little to say, and if ever teased about Waubenoo he fell into a great passion.

"Waubenoo herself was too sensible to gratify their idle curiosity, but the very return of her brightness, and her unwillingness to talk about the matter, only added to the foolish desires of outsiders to find out what had really occurred. So some of these naughty busybodies began questioning the children when they could get them away from Waubenoo, for in her presence they were as mute as she was. They pestered and bothered the children and tried in various ways before they succeeded. But one day, while Waubenoo was away overhauling her traps, some of those wicked meddlers visited her wigwam and succeeded in getting one of the smallest ones--I just forget now whether it was a boy or a girl."

"A girl, of course," shouted Sagastao.

"No, indeed; I am sure it was a naughty boy," said Minnehaha.

"Well, no matter which; but one of them said: 'Nanahboozhoo!'

"This one word, Nanahboozhoo, was quite enough to startle and alarm them, for Nanahboozhoo was also much feared, as he sometimes did dreadful things.

"The fact that Nanahboozhoo had been in their very midst, although they were a long time in hearing anything more than the one word from the now frightened children, was quite enough to excite the whole village, for the news was soon spread abroad by the tattlers.

"Such busybodies could not be satisfied with only hearing that Nanahboozhoo had visited the wigwam of Waubenoo. Of course they wanted to hear about what he said and did, and I am sorry to have to say that after a while, with coaxing and presents, they managed to get from the children the whole delightfully exciting story.

"When Gray Wolf, who was so jeered and laughed at by all who dare, heard from the gossipers how it had happened that he had received such a thrashing he was doubly wild and furious.

"When Waubenoo found out that all was known about how Nanahboozhoo had helped her she was very sorry that her little brothers and sisters had been so naughty and disobedient. She also knew that now she would have to be more careful than ever against the movements of Gray Wolf. But the fact was that he had been so cowed by his beating that he was afraid to openly attack her, lest she should get Nanahboozhoo to help her again and it might be worse for him than it was at his first meeting. But he treasured up revengeful feelings in his heart and resolved that at some time or other he would dreadfully punish her.

"Some years passed by, and the older children, next to Waubenoo, were able to do most of the hunting and fishing as well as to be on guard against any of the evil doings of Gray Wolf. Thus they were able, in a measure, to repay their sister, whom they dearly loved, although they were so thoughtless, for all her great kindness to them.

"One fall there came to the village a splendid Indian hunter. He was of the same tribe, but lived with his people, most of the time, at a distant part of the country. He was so pleased with this village, where dwelt Waubenoo, that he decided to remain for the winter and hunt. He was such a very pleasant fellow and such a great hunter that he soon made many friends. Gray Wolf was the only man who seemed to hate him, and he was even so rash as to insult him openly in an Indian gathering.

"Soquaatum, for this was the young warrior's name, stood the insults of Gray Wolf for some time, then, when he saw that some of the young hunters began to think he was afraid of Gray Wolf, he suddenly sprang at him and knocked him down, and then seizing him by his belt, he shook him as easily and thoroughly as a wildcat would a rabbit. Then he threw him from him and sat down among the people as though nothing had happened.

"That evening, when he and the relatives with whom he lived were seated around the fire in the wigwam, he heard for the first time the story of Waubenoo: of her great industry, her love for her little brothers and sisters, and how she had been threatened by Gray Wolf and then befriended by Nanahboozhoo.

"This story very much interested Soquaatum, and especially as in his hunting he had met her younger brother, now a fine strapping hunter, and had become very fond of him, although he was much younger. So he resolved that as soon as he could he would visit her wigwam and seek her acquaintance."

"Ho! Ho! So this is to be a love story," said Sagastao.

"Be quiet, do," said his sister. "All love stories do not end well. Remember, there was Gray Wolf!"

Souwanas profited by the interruption, for it gave him an opportunity to light his pipe with flint and steel, and he then resumed the story.

"Soon after Soquaatum arrayed himself in his most attractive costume and called at the tent of Waubenoo. His excuse was that he wanted to see her brother and arrange some hunting excursion.

"Waubenoo, who had often heard her brother speak of his great skill as a hunter, and had also heard how easily and thoroughly he had handled Gray Wolf, received him most kindly and at once made him welcome.

"Well, it is not surprising that he should soon fall in love with Waubenoo, and so pleased was she with his manner, as well as his attractive appearance, that she became very fond of him, and it was not many days after their first meeting before it was noised abroad that Soquaatum and Waubenoo were lovers.

"Soquaatum remained until about the middle of the winter. Then he returned to his distant home to make all preparations for receiving his wife, for whom he was to come in the spring.

"Gray Wolf was, of course, furious when he heard that Waubenoo was to be married, and to the man who had humiliated him in the presence of so many people. Though angry and revengeful, he was at heart a cowardly fellow, and now that Waubenoo's brother was full-grown he was afraid of him, as well as of Soquaatum while he was in the neighborhood. But his fears did not prevent him from thinking of schemes for revenge which, however, came to nothing, because the friends of Waubenoo were so vigilant and well prepared.

"At length one of his plans succeeded, and this is how it happened:

"Gray Wolf enlisted a young Indian who was equally bad with himself to help him. As Soquaatum had now been gone for some weeks to his home, which was far east from that region, Gray Wolf and his wicked companion went a good long distance--many miles--in that direction. There they made a hunting lodge and laid their plans to capture Waubenoo. Then Gray Wolf's companion went back and remained secreted near the wigwam of Waubenoo. One night he saw her two brothers leave, about midnight, for some distant traps that would take them all day to reach.

"As soon as this bad fellow was satisfied that they were well out of sight and hearing he rushed up to the tent of Waubenoo and hastily aroused her from her sleep. He had arrayed himself as though he was gaining on her, she began calling: 'Soquaatum! Soquaatum!' Alas! he was far away, but there was another who, fortunately, was near. Nanahboozhoo had been out hunting and he had a sled which he was dragging, loaded with game. He was surprised as he heard this calling, 'Soquaatum! Soquaatum!' and as he continued listening it became hoarse and then only like a whisper. He could stand it no longer; he rushed through the woods and there he saw Waubenoo, dashing along on snow-shoes, calling in a low whisper: 'Soquaatum! Soquaatum!' while not a hundred feet behind her was Gray Wolf, yelling in triumph that he would soon capture her. Unfortunately Nanahboozhoo was not in a very good humor that day. He had heard of some little children that had been tattling about him, and he had heard that the children in the tent of Waubenoo had told about his visit.

"However, when he saw who it was that was in danger, and heard her cry to him for help when she saw him, and especially when he saw who it was that was after her, he quickly turned Waubenoo into a bird and without any trouble she quickly flew up into a tree out of the reach of danger.

"Ever since that Waubenoo has been the Whisky Jack, and if you will listen to Whisky Jack when he is not scolding or clamoring at your camp for food his voice is like that of the lost Indian maiden, with a bad cold, calling for her lover."

"What did Nanahboozhoo do to Gray Wolf?" said Sagastao.

"Hush," said Minnehaha. "Don't you know Nanahboozhoo doesn't like to have children talk about him?"

This excessive caution on the part of the little girl vastly amused Souwanas. Then he told them that Nanahboozhoo turned Gray Wolf into a dog and made him draw home his heavy load of meat.

CHAPTER XV.

A Novel Race: the Wolverine and the Rock--How the Wolverine's Legs were Shortened--A Punishment for Conceit.

There was great excitement one morning among the children in the school-room when Mary came in with the word that some hunters with their dog sleds had called, and that they had with them a great wolverine which had been killed in the woods not very far away. The children ran out to look at it.

Now the wolverine is known to be such a cunning, clever animal that the killing of one is quite an event among the Indians, and the lucky hunter who succeeds in destroying one is the hero of the hour. A man may on one hunting trip kill several bears or wolves, or many other animals, and there is not much said about it, but to kill a wolverine, that pest and scourge of the hunters, is indeed a feat that any man is proud of.

"Why is it called a wolverine?" asked Sagastao.

"Because it was once like a wolf, and had small feet and long legs, but now its legs are short and its feet are very large."

"What shortened its legs and made its feet become so large?" asked Sagastao.

It was too cold a day to remain any longer outside looking at the wolverine, or to learn more about it, so the children were obliged to return to their warm school-room, where their lessons were resumed.

It was evident, however, that both Sagastao and Minnehaha were ready with a couple of questions for Mary, and it was not long after school hours that they sought her and asked:

"Mary, what was it that shortened the legs of the wolverine? and what made his feet so big?"

"The wolverine," replied Mary, "was once the finest of all the different kinds of wolves. He had the softest and nicest of fur. His legs were long, and his feet were firm and handsome, but he was an awfully conceited fellow. He fancied he was the handsomest creature in existence and looked down with contempt on all the other kinds of wolves. He used to go to the side of the clear transparent lake, where he could see his shadow reflected in the water, and he would strut up and down and say: 'O dear, what a lovely creature I am!'

"It is true he was very clever in many ways. He was so swift that he could run down even the antelope and the elk, and at all the great animal gatherings, where the different creatures met in council, he was the swiftest there, and easily won the chief prizes at the great races which the animals used to hold. Indeed, he won so many races that at length he could get no animal to compete with him. He even tried to get up races with the birds, but they laughed at him for his conceit.

"One day he happened to be hunting among the mountains. Near the top of one he saw a large ball-like rock, standing there apart from the other big rocks. Coming up close to this great round rock he said to it:

"'Was that you I saw walking just now?'

"'No; I cannot walk, I have lain here for a long time,' said the rock.

"The wolverine retorted that he was sure he had seen the rock walking.

"This made the rock angry and he told the wolverine that he was telling a falsehood. Then the saucy wolverine replied:

"'You need not speak to me in that way, for I have seen you walking.'

"Then the wolverine ran off a little distance and challenged the rock to catch him. But the rock did not reply to this and the bold wolverine came close up to the rock, struck it with his paw, and said:

"'Come, now, see if you can catch me!'

"'I cannot run,' said the rock, 'but I can roll.'

"At this the conceited wolverine began to laugh. 'That will do! All I want is a race. You can run or roll, just as you like.'

"Then the race began; the wolverine started down the mountain side at a great rate, and the rock came rolling behind him. At first the big rock did not move very fast, and the wolverine laughed as he looked back and saw the rock was so far behind. But the rock came on faster and faster, and now it made the wolverine do his very best to keep ahead of it. On they rushed, over the sticks and stones and rough places, down--down that great, long mountain side. At length, swift and strong as he was, the wolverine began to get tired, and although he was running as he never did before in his life the big rock was surely gaining on him. By and by he was so frightened that in looking behind at the rock, now close at his heels, he tripped over a stick and down he fell. The rock rolled over him and, just as it had completely crushed him down to the earth, there it stopped.

"Then the wolverine, whose head was not crushed under the rock, cried out:

"'Get off! go away! you are hurting me. You are crushing my bones.'

"But the rock replied:

"'You tormented me and told me I was telling a falsehood, and you challenged me to a race with you; and now that I have caught you I will not stir until some one stronger comes and takes me off.'

"Then the wolverine lifted up his voice and cried to his relatives, the wolves and foxes, to come and remove the rock.

"When these animals came and saw him in such a plight, they asked him:

"'How came you to get under the rock?'

"The wolverine replied:

"'I challenged the rock to catch me, and it rolled on me.'

"When the wolves and the foxes heard this they were not very sorry. They knew how conceited the wolverine had been about his speed, indeed they were all smarting because of the ease with which he had beaten them, and so, instead of helping him at once, they said he deserved his punishment.

"After a time, however, they began to be sorry for the poor wolverine, who was crying out piteously for help, but they found they were not able to remove the rock. They could not even stir it in the least.

"'Get out of the way,' said the wolverine, 'and I will call my other friends, the thunder and the lightning.'

"In a few minutes a great black cloud was seen rapidly coming out of the west. As it came rushing along the foxes and the wolves were very much frightened by the great noise it made. However, they had courage enough to ask the lightning to take off the fine coat of the wolverine but not to kill him. Then they ran back and watched to see the lightning do its work. The lightning promised to do what had been asked of him; for he had heard of this proud, conceited wolverine, who had boasted that he could run like lightning, and now he was just going to teach him a lesson. So he darted back a distance to gather force, and then he came on with a rush and struck the rock and knocked it into small pieces. He also completely stripped the skin from the back of the wolverine but did not kill him. When the wolverine got up and stood there naked, with all his beauty gone, he was very angry at the lightning.

"'You are like other so-called friends I have heard about,' he said; 'you cannot do a thing but you must overdo it and spoil all. You had no need to tear my beautiful fur coat from my back when you knew I only asked you to come and strike the rock.'

"Then the poor, shivering wolverine gathered the pieces of his coat and carried them to his sister the frog, who dwelt in a marsh, and he asked her to sew them together. The frog had sore eyes, and when she sewed them together she did not do it properly. Hence the wolverine was very angry, and he hit her a crack on the head and knocked her into the water. Then he took up the coat and went and found his youngest sister, the mouse. He told her of his troubles, and how the frog had so badly done her work. Then he showed the mouse how he wanted the coat to be sewed. His little sister felt badly for her big brother, and so she set to work and with great care sewed all the pieces together in their right places. When the wolverine saw how nicely she had done her work he was much pleased.

"'You mice may live everywhere,' he said, in real gratitude, 'and in spite of all your enemies you will never be destroyed.'

"Then the wolverine tried to put on his coat, but, alas! he found his legs had been shortened and his feet very much flattened out by the terrible crushing he had had under that big stone which he had been so foolish as to challenge to a race."

"Guess he didn't run many more races," said Sagastao.

"No, indeed," was the reply; "he was so mortified and angry that from that day to this the wolverine has always been a sulking, solitary animal, and playing all the mean tricks he can on all kinds of animals as though he had a spite against them. He now has not one friend who ever cares for him, unless it is his little sister the mouse."

CHAPTER XVI.

The Legend of the Twin Children of the Sun--How They Rid the Earth of Some of the Great Monsters--Their Great Battle with Nikoochis, the Giant.

One pleasant summer day, when the children had the pleasure of a canoe outing with Mary and Kennedy, they decided to visit the wigwam of their old friends, Kinnesasis and his wife. They had not seen them for some time, and as Souwanas was away on a long hunting excursion they could not expect any Nanahboozhoo stories until his return. Kinnesasis was a capital story-teller, and they were eager to reach his wigwam. There, after making both him and his wife happy with some gifts, they knew they could get some interesting stories in return.

They met with a hearty welcome and spent a happy day there. Among the stories Kinnesasis told them, as handed down by his forefathers, the following is perhaps the most interesting:

"Long ago there were great monsters on this earth. Some of them were enormous animals and fiercer than any that now exist. Then there were magicians, and other evil spirits, like windegoos, some of whom were tall, giant cannibals, that filled the people with terror. They lay in wait and caught the children, and even the grown-up people, as the wild beasts now catch their prey. Then they kindled up great fires and roasted them and ate them.

"Often, when the parents went to look for their children, they also were caught and eaten.

"The people were rendered very miserable not only by these great monsters in human form, but also by the attacks of the enormous animals that then lived. Indeed they began to fear that they would all soon be killed, unless help came to them.

"These people were worshipers of the sun, whom they called the great Sun Father, and some tribes still have their sun dances in his honor. When he saw that the people were in such great trouble and were likely to be all killed by their cruel enemies he resolved to deliver them from their foes. So he disguised himself and came down to the earth and married a beautiful woman of the Northland. They had lovely twin boys, whose names were Sesigizit, the older, and Ooseemeeid, the younger. They grew so rapidly that they were able to walk when only a few days old. Their sun father disappeared as soon as they were born, going to the far East-land.

"Strange to say, although these two boys grew so rapidly at first, they as suddenly ceased growing, and so remained quite small. But they were very intelligent, and were ever asking questions.

"'Who is our father?'" they inquired of their mother one day.

But she ignored the question, and although they kept bothering her it was a long time before she would give them any information at all, and that was very little. However, she did tell them that they were more than ordinary children and finer than other boys, but then there are lots of mothers who say such things to their own little ones.

"As they were now big enough, she brought out of hiding a couple of bows, and quivers full of arrows, and some magic rabbit sticks, and gave them to the boys.

"'These were left for you by your father,' said the mother, ere he went away, 'and he gave commands that they were to be given to you as soon as you were able to use them.'

"The children were, of course, anxious to try their bows and arrows and these magic sticks. So very soon after they had received them they resolved to go off on a hunting expedition.

"The mother, who was anxious about them, warned them of the various monsters in human shape, great windegoos and cannibals, that were ever lying in wait to catch and roast and eat little boys. She also told them of the animals that were so enormously large that they could catch them up and swallow them as easily as a turkey does a grasshopper.

"Thus she tried to put them on their guard against the terrible foes that had devoured so many of their people. The boys, however, were not much frightened, and they eagerly set off on their journey.

"They were especially warned by their anxious mother not to go to the east, as there was a narrow lake there to which many of these evil creatures came for water, especially a great monster wolf that had devoured many people. Yet they immediately started off in that direction, for, like some other boys, they did not obey even their mother. It was noon before they reached the lake. At first, as they examined it, everything seemed very quiet and still.

"'Mother must have been mistaken,' said Sesigizit; 'I do not see any living thing here.'

"But as they wandered farther along the shore, suddenly Ooseemeeid cried out:

"'O see that great wolf on the other side!'

"They dropped down as quickly as they could, but the fierce brute had already caught sight of them. He was very much larger than any of the wolves that now howl in the dark forests. He not only destroyed many of the people, but when he came to springs, or small streams, he either drank up all the water or so spoiled it that it was unfit for use.

"The boys shot their arrows at him, but his sides were so tough, for he had bones like jointed armor upon them, that he was only slightly wounded. He was, however, made very angry by their attacks, and he picked up a magic stick and threw it at them. They would have fared badly if they had not so suddenly thrown themselves upon the ground that it passed over them.

"When the boys saw that their arrows were not swift enough to kill such a great animal they decided to use the magic rabbit sticks which their father, the sun, had given them, with orders that they were only to be used when the arrows failed.

"The wolf, when he saw that one of his magic sticks had missed its aim, was more savage than ever, and he seized his remaining one, for he only had two, and he threw it with all his power at the boys. This time they both jumped high up from the ground and the stick passed under them.

"It was their turn now, and so they both threw their magic sticks with such force that the great bony armor of the wolf was crushed in and he was killed.

"Sesigizit quickly ran around the lake to the spot where the great body lay and cut out the heart of the wolf, while Ooseemeeid secured the two magic sticks that the wolf had thrown at them, as well as their own weapons, and then with these trophies they returned to their own home.

"'Where have you been?' asked the anxious mother when they appeared.

"'We have been to the lake,' they replied.

"She could hardly believe it.

"'My boys,' she said, 'you surely are mistaken, for no one who goes there returns. The great monsters that devour our people live there, and they let no one escape.'

"Then they told her of their battle with the great wolf, and how they had killed him. They also showed her his heart, which they had brought home with them.

"She was very much excited. She called the people together, and there was great rejoicing at the death of this terrible wolf which had been such a scourge to them.

"Some time after Sesigizit and Ooseemeeid asked their mother if she knew where grew any good tough wood suitable for making bows and arrows. Her answer was:

"'Far away in the foothills is a canyon, or ravine, where a forest of just such wood as you need is growing, but the path that leads to it is narrow, and there sits guard a great monster giant who kills and throws into the ravine everyone who has attempted to get any of that wood. And in addition there is a fierce mountain lioness prowling around somewhere on the route, and she has already killed many people and carried them off to her den.'

"Ooseemeeid at once desired to set off and get a supply of this wood, but Sesigizit, when he found out how fearful their mother was that they would both be killed if they made the attempt, at first refused to go. His objection, however, vanished when he saw his brother making ready to start, and in spite of their mother's fears they started off.

"They had not gone very far when they met the great mountain lioness. She was out hunting food for her cubs. These she had hidden in a den which was away up on a precipitous mountain side.

"Ooseemeeid asked her if she knew the way to the canyon where grew the good wood.

"'Yes,' she replied. 'I am just going that way, and I will show you the route.' She said this because she wished in this way to allure the two boys to walk near to her den, and there she would kill them for food for her cubs.

"So she led them until they came to a place where the path was very dangerous, because it was on a narrow, shelving rock around the mountain side. Here the monster lioness asked the boys to walk on ahead of her, but they refused, saying that they had been taught never to walk in front of their elders. The lioness urged, but the boys were firm, and so she had to yield and let them have their way.

"When in the most dangerous part of the pass the boys pretended to be very much alarmed, and asked to be permitted to walk between her and the mountain side. At first she was suspicious, but they seemed now to be so cowardly and afraid that she thought they were not able to do her any harm, so she walked on the outer edge of the pass and let them have the inside, and also allowed them to put their hands on her as though to steady themselves. When they came to the most dangerous spot, where it was so narrow that even a mountain lion had to be careful, they both suddenly drew their magic sticks and, giving her a great shove, sent her over the side of the narrow rocky ledge and down she fell--to be dashed to pieces thousands of feet below.

"With a shout of triumph the two boys carefully pushed on and, finding the den, quickly killed the cubs and cut off the right forepaw from each one to carry home.

"From this high pass they could now see the canyon where grew the good wood for which they were seeking. They also saw the lodge of the monster giant who guarded the narrow path that led to it. They saw by its size that he must be an enormous creature, and so they looked to see that their arrows and magic sticks were all in good order and handy for use.

"The great giant had heard their shout of triumph when they had destroyed the mountain lioness and it made him very angry, for he hated any noise or disturbance; his name, Nikoochis, which means solitude, indicated this.

"When he saw the small boys he was at first inclined to laugh in derision at them, but when they had come near enough to shoot their magic arrows at him he soon began to roar with the stinging pain they gave him.

"In vain he tried to catch the active little fellows; he was so big and clumsy, and they were so quick in their movements, that it was an utter impossibility for him to get his hands upon them.

"Then he began tearing up great rocks and stones and tried to crush them by hurling these at them. Here the boys' father, the sun, came to their help, and he shone so fiercely into the eyes of the great monster that he was unable to see very well, and the boys easily kept out of the way of the rocks thrown at them.

"The monster was big and fat and unaccustomed to exertion, and he was soon tired out. Indeed he was so big that the arrows of the boys seemed only like pins and needles sticking into him, and the boys began to fear that their quivers would be emptied before they had conquered him. Just then they met an old witch with a bundle of sticks which she was carrying to her wigwam. She was very angry with Nikoochis, for he would not allow her even to gather the dry sticks that fell to the ground in the forest he was guarding. The result was that she had to wander far away to get the little fuel she needed in her wigwam.

"The boys told her of their battle with this selfish old monster, and that even now he was badly wounded by their arrows, which, however, did not seem to reach any vital spot. She told them that the only place where their weapons could be effectual in killing him was in the top of his skull. That they must first in some way crack it with their magic rabbit sticks, and then they could shoot their arrows into his brain. Hearing this they quickly resumed their attack upon him. In vain he tore up great rocks and hurled them with all his force at them. They either cleverly jumped on one side or sprang up into the air out of the way.

"Then, watching for their opportunity, they waited until he stooped down, and when he was struggling to loosen from the earth a great rock as big as a house Sesigizit threw, with all his power, his magic rabbit stick. It struck the giant fair on the top of his head with such force that it broke off a piece of his skull. The next instant Ooseemeeid fired one of his arrows so accurately that it pierced into the brain through the spot thus left exposed.

"With a roar of rage and pain the great monster fell, rolled down into the deep canyon, and died.

"After securing his big flint knife, which dropped from his belt, the boys hurried into the canyon and gathered a lot of fine wood for arrow shafts and returned to their mother. When she asked them where they had been they replied that they had been to the canyon, and that they had killed both the mountain lioness and the great giant.

"At first she could hardly believe this, but as they had brought the paws of the cubs and the flint knife of the great giant, why, she just had to believe it. Great indeed were the rejoicings of the people at being thus rid of these creatures."

CHAPTER XVII.

Souwanas Tells of the Queer Way in which Nanahboozhoo Destroyed Mooshekinnebik, the Last of the Great Monsters.

One cold day Souwanas, who had not been seen by the children for some time--he had been away on a long hunting excursion--quite unexpectedly walked into the mission house during the school hours of Sagastao and Minnehaha. The news of his coming was hailed with delight by the children, and it required a certain amount of firmness on the part of the heads of the household to keep them at their studies. They were, however, quickly pacified, and returned with diligence to their lessons, when informed that their old friend had been invited to stay all day and doubtless would have a story of some kind for them when their studies were all over.

The venison and bear's meat which he had brought were quickly purchased at a price that well pleased him. Then he sat down for a rest and a smoke in the kitchen. Of course he had his usual tiff with Mary, the nurse, who was very jealous of him because he had so won the love and confidence of the children. Souwanas was greatly amused at her jealousy of him, especially since he was told by one of the Indian maids that the children had been overheard gravely debating between themselves which was the better story-teller, Mary or Souwanas.

When peace again reigned some illustrated volumes from the library were given to Souwanas for his inspection. He was not able to read English, but he was very fond of looking at pictures.

There was one book that had a special fascination for him, in fact when he first examined it, and had had some of its illustrations explained to him, it gave this superstitious Indian about the biggest fright he had ever received. It was a book in which were pictured and described many of the great extinct monsters of the old times. These enormous hideous creatures, whose bones and fossil remains are still occasionally to be found, quite alarmed him. Yet the book was generally about the first one he desired to see.

On this present visit, however, Souwanas, while as usual eager again to inspect this book, was observed to look at it in a very different spirit. The explanation came out later, when he had the children around him--indeed almost the whole household--listening to a new Nanahboozhoo story which he had secured from some famous old Indian whom he had met while far away on his long hunting excursion.

"Yes, it is true," he began, "that there did once live on this earth, both in the land and in the water, great animals like those here shown in this book. I have been to the wigwam of the great Shuniou and from him I have learned much about them, as handed down in the tradition of our forefathers. Great and terrible were they, and the people of those times lived in great terror of them, for the bows and arrows and even the stone war clubs of the strongest warriors were powerless to kill or even dangerously wound such monsters. It was well for the inhabitants of the earth in those days that these great monsters were few in number and that they were constantly fighting among themselves, for so large and terrible were they that only animals as big and fierce of other kinds could battle with them.

"But there was one great monster that lived in the water, and as he had no enemies big enough to attack him he lived on, even long after the other great animals were all killed off.

"Shuniou said that the tradition was that a great rush of waters caused many of the last of the great monsters that had tusks of ivory to be carried to the far Northland, and there, as the terribly cold winter set in, they were all frozen to death.

"This must be true," added Souwanas, "for it was not many years ago that the Hudson Bay Company sent their men there to get this ivory, which they intended to ship to England. They came back with word that some of the dead bodies had been seen where the ice broke up. But this great monster in the water, as I have said, lived on after the rest were all supposed to have died off or been killed. He was a terrible scourge to those Indians whose wigwams were on the shores of the great sea in which he lived. They were in mortal terror when they ventured out in their canoes to fish. This they had to do, as they depended almost entirely on fish for their living, and there were times when the fish left the shallow waters near the shore and went out far from land. There the Indians had to follow and catch them or they and their families would starve.

"Happily for them, sometimes for months together no one would hear or see anything of this great sea monster. Then, perhaps, suddenly he would rise up right under a canoe in which were several Indians, whom he would easily catch and swallow one by one. He would sometimes rush after a herd of deer that had gone out swimming in the waters. He would catch and easily swallow several of them."

"Well, I should think that the big horns of a moose or reindeer would give him some trouble to swallow," said Sagastao.

"He was so large," said Souwanas, "that the horns or body of the largest deer did not seem to bother him in the least degree."

"I wonder if it were not one of his great grandfathers that swallowed Jonah," said the observant Minnehaha.

"The Indians at length came to be so much distressed by the loss of so many of their number, and by their inability to slay the monster, that they resolved to ask Nanahboozhoo to come and help them if he possibly could.

"I ought to have told you," said Souwanas, "that this great monster was called by the Indians Mooshekinnebik.

"Nanahboozhoo at once responded to their request, for he was very angry when he heard how many industrious fishermen had been swallowed by this creature. He was doubly angry when he returned with the deputation who had gone for him and further learned that, only the day before, Mooshekinnebik had been mean enough to come near to the shore and catch and swallow some boys and girls who had been out swimming that warm summer day.

"When Nanahboozhoo informed Nokomis of the request of the people for his help to deliver them from the long hated Mooshekinnebik she was very much frightened, and more so when he told her of the strange and dangerous plan he was going to adopt to carry out his purpose. It was this: he was going to allow himself to be swallowed by this monster who had already destroyed so many people."

"O how dreadful!" said Minnehaha. "We will never hear any more nice stories about Nanahboozhoo."

"All a pack of lies; there never were any such monsters," snapped out old Mary, who could not longer conceal her jealousy at seeing how interested the children were in the story.

"Hold on, Mary; not so fast," cried Sagastao, taking the book from Souwanas and showing the pictures to Mary.

"There, Sakehow," he said, using his favorite term of endearment, "look for yourself and see those lovely creatures--some of them quite big enough to swallow us all without winking."

But Mary was stubborn, as well as jealous, and would not give in, even when Kennedy, the favorite dog driver, who was present, told her that even now there were some of the great tusks and bones of animals that the officers called mammoths over at the Hudson Bay Company's fort ready to be shipped to England next summer. She was, however, quickly silenced when Sagastao sat down beside her and throwing his head into her lap said, very coaxingly:

"Now, Mary, just be quiet and let us hear Souwanas tell the rest of the story of what Nanahboozhoo did to Mooshekinnebik."

Peace being thus restored, Souwanas, who had been much amused by Mary's ire, resumed his story:

"When Nokomis heard her grandson describe how he was going to let the monster swallow him she resolved to come and pitch her tent on the seashore, among the people who had been so troubled, and there to await the return of her grandson, if he should ever come back from such a perilous adventure.

"Nanahboozhoo asked his mother for some magic singing sticks, and also for a very sharp knife. Then he made for himself a small raft of logs and, bidding her good-bye for a short time, he sprang on it and was soon floating out, in search of the dreaded creature, over the great waters.

"When well out from the shore he began to make music with his magic sticks and to sing a defiant song:

"'Ho, ho! great fish down in the sea,   Come, if you dare, and swallow me.   My brothers all you're fond of eating,   'Tis time some one gave you a beating.   He, he! Hi, hi! Ho, ho! Ho, ho!

"'You see I am not far away,   So come and taste me while you may;   Yet not afraid am I, no, no!   So hurry up, old fish. Ho, ho!   He, he! Hi, hi! Ho, ho! Ho, ho!'

"Nanahboozhoo sang this brave song over and over, to the weird harmony of his magic music sticks, until he reached the place where the great fish was resting.

"When the great monster Mooshekinnebik heard the voice of Nanahboozhoo he came up to the surface of the water to find out who was making all that music and shouting out such defiant words.

"When he saw that it was only one young man on a raft of dry logs, he ordered one of his children to go and knock the raft to pieces and swallow that noisy fellow. But this was not what Nanahboozhoo wanted, and so he shouted out:

"'I want the old father fish to eat me.'

"This made old Mooshekinnebik very angry, and so, open mouthed, he rushed furiously at Nanahboozhoo who, when the great monster was close enough, took a leap into the open mouth and was immediately swallowed up.

"For a short time after being swallowed Nanahboozhoo was unconscious, but he soon recovered himself and was able to look around and see the queer prison in which he was now confined. It was fortunate for him that he had eyes like a cat, and so could see as well in the dark as in the light. He found that he was not the only inmate of this queer prison; there were a lot of creatures whom he called his brothers--the bear, the deer, the fox, the beaver and even the squirrel. Nanahboozhoo inquired of them and they told him how they had been captured and the length of time they had been in that horrid place. They also informed him that many others who had been captured were now dead. Nanahboozhoo found that they were quite hopeless, and looked forward to nothing but death. However he called them around him and informed them that he had willingly come among them for the purpose of affording a speedy deliverance.

"This was indeed good news. Then he explained to them the plan he had in his mind, and said that it was necessary for them to kick up a rumpus in the interior of this monster, that they would thus make him so very sick that he would have to go near to land, and when they should have him there he thought he had another plan that would enable them all to escape.

"They all agreed to do anything they could to help on his plans, so Nanahboozhoo took out his magic singing sticks and began to play and sing.

"At once the bear, the deer, the fox, the beaver, and indeed all of the creatures that were still alive, caught up the lively tune, and such a dancing and jumping and flying around was hardly ever seen before.

"This internal commotion very much disturbed Mooshekinnebik. He could not make out what was the matter. He shook himself thoroughly, but that did no good; then he darted off through the water at a great rate, but this also was of no use. Then he rolled over and over and over in the water. This of course stopped the dancing and hubbub inside for a time, but as the walls of the prison were soft, also the floor and ceiling, nobody was hurt, and so the instant it ceased they were up and at it again, harder than ever. Mooshekinnebik never had such a turn in his life. He did not know what to do. Still Nanahboozhoo kept singing louder and louder, while the dancers kept up their wild antics around him.

"At length Nanahboozhoo decided that the monster was about enough frightened for him to do something else, and so he drew out his sharp knife and gave Mooshekinnebik a good stab near his heart.

"This threw him into convulsions and added to his terror, and he began swimming toward the shore. When Nanahboozhoo knew this he kept stabbing him more and more, until at length his body was heard to scrape on the shallow sandy ground. At this Nanahboozhoo with a mighty effort plunged his knife with all his power deep into the monster's heart.

"The instant he did this Mooshekinnebik was thrown into a number of mighty convulsions, and in one of them, with one tremendous effort, he fairly threw himself out of the water on the shore, and there he died.

"So great and terrible had been these dying convulsions that all the creatures inside, and even Nanahboozhoo himself, had become unconscious from being so knocked about.

"How long they remained so they did not know. Nanahboozhoo was the first to regain his senses, and he was indeed very sorry to see that all of his comrades were still unconscious. He had some difficulty in getting out from under the bodies of his comrades, who were piled up on him. He was glad that the monster was dead, but he was uncertain whether they were on the shore or at the bottom of the water. So he speedily determined to find out. He climbed up over the bodies of his comrades to the place that he thought was the thinnest, and there, with his keen knife, he began cutting through the roof of this queer prison.

"To his great delight he was soon able to see the sunshine coming through. When he had cut a hole big enough to let in some air and sunshine he took up his magic singing sticks and began singing, for the purpose of reviving all those imprisoned with him. His song was not much to us, but it was a great deal to those shut up in such a prison. It was:

"'Kesik-in-na-win, Kesik-in-na-win.' (I see the sky, I see the sky.)

"As Nanahboozhoo continued to sing this over and over, one after another his brothers sneezed and opened their eyes. They were indeed a happy lot at the prospect of deliverance.

"When Nanahboozhoo saw that they were all now recovered he again set to work with his knife, and it was not long before he had a hole large enough to permit all of the imprisoned creatures to make their escape.

"The news soon spread, and it was not long before Nokomis, with others, came to see the huge dead monster, and there were great rejoicings."

"And this," added Souwanas, "is the tradition, as told by Shuniou, of how Nanahboozhoo destroyed Mooshekinnebik."

"What became of the little monsters?" asked Minnehaha.

"The Indians," replied Souwanas, "under the leadership of Nanahboozhoo made such a war upon them that they were soon annihilated."

CHAPTER XVIII.

Welcome Springtime in the Northland--How Nanahboozhoo Killed the Great White Sea Lion, the Chief of the Magicians--The Revenge--The Flood--Escape of Nanahboozhoo and the Animals on the Raft--The Creation of a New World.

The coming of the pleasant springtime was hailed with great delight. Seven or eight months were found to be a very long spell of cold winter weather, and so when with a rapidity unknown in more Southern climates the winter broke up, and the welcome warm weather made its appearance, everybody seemed to feel its genial influence.

The first little wild flowers were looked for with intense interest, and great indeed was the joy of the children when some were found. The sweet singing birds that in the previous autumn, on the first signs of the coming down from the colder North of the Frost King, had flitted away to the summer Southland were now returning in multitudes. The air was full of their melody, and as scores of them, fearless and trustful, made themselves at home in the bird resorts around Wahkiegum, great indeed was the children's delight as they welcomed them back to their haunts in the North.

And really it did seem as though the birds were glad to be there again, for it is only in the North that these birds sing their sweet love songs to each other and build their nests and hatch out their little broods.

The Whisky Jacks, that had been croaking out their hoarse cries all winter, seemed to get sulky and vexed that they were now so little admired, and so they flitted away farther north and buried themselves in the interior of the deepest forests.

In the joyousness of those happy days up in those high latitudes, when the changes of every twenty-four hours can easily be noticed, Sagastao and Minnehaha for a time troubled neither Souwanas nor Mary for Indian legends or stories. There was in the rapid melting of the snow, the breaking up of the immense ice fields on the lake, the appearance of the land, and then the grass and flowers, and the planting of seeds in their little gardens, enough to keep them busy and happy.

But even all these things at length lost their interest. The flights of the wild geese, swans, and ducks had all ceased. They, with many other kinds of migrating birds, were busy nesting. The sweet songsters around the home were everyday companions, and, while the children loved them as much as ever, the excitement of their coming had died away. So when one day they saw Souwanas coming over the now sparkling waters in his canoe they were delighted to welcome him. As usual, when he reached the shore the contents of his canoe were examined speedily. There the children found a couple of beavers that had but lately been trapped, and a dozen or more muskrats that Souwanas had speared in the marshes. These animals were the result of one night's hunting, and now Souwanas was on his way home to have them skinned and the pelts prepared for sale to the fur traders.

The children's curiosity was much aroused by the sight of the beavers and muskrats, and they questioned the old man about them. The queer, broad, scaly tail of the beavers much interested them, and drew from Souwanas an interesting account of the various purposes for which the clever, industrious beavers use this apparently awkward appendage.

"Do you know any Nanahboozhoo stories in which he tells anything about beavers or muskrats?" asked Sagastao.

"Yes, indeed," replied Souwanas; "in nearly all the stories that are told about the forming of the new land after the great flood both the beaver and the muskrat are mentioned, as well as the other animals."

"Tell us one of the stories," urged little Minnehaha.

The arrival of some other canoes at this point interrupted the conversation. The newcomers were on their way to the wigwam of Souwanas, who was their chief. He was about to go on with them, but when he saw the look of disappointment on the faces of the children he, with his usual thoughtful kindness, transferred the two beavers and the muskrats from his own canoe to one of the late arrivals. Then telling the people to give them to his wife, to have them all cooked and ready for dinner, by which time he would join them, he sent the people on their way. Having lighted his calumet, with the children seated near him, he began:

"Nanahboozhoo's life commenced long before the great flood of waters that covered the earth, about which all of our tribes have heard something. He had his own wigwam and furnished it with everything he wanted. One day when walking on the shore of a great river he saw some sea lions lying on the sandy beach, basking in the sun. These animals, like the beaver, could live as well in the water as on the land. As he closely watched them from a distance, and saw the rich, shiny skins, he thought what a nice tobacco pouch could be made out of one of them. When Nanahboozhoo once set his heart on anything he at once began to work hard to secure it. He tried various plans to capture one of these sea-lions, but none of them succeeded. They were too clever to be caught as other animals are, and he saw that he would have to adopt some unusual method. He decided that he would go down very early to the spot on the bank of the river where they were in the habit of sunning themselves and disguise himself as an old stump of a tree, then, when they came out and were enjoying the sunshine, he would shoot the fine old white one with the beautiful glossy skin that he had so much admired. As on other days the lions came, and when they saw this stump the white lion, which was a kind of king among them, said:

"'I never saw that big stump before. I think it must be Nanahboozhoo.'

"Another one said he thought the same thing.

"Others only laughed, and said, 'It is only an old pine stump.'

"However, as a number of them were suspicious, it was decided to go up and shake it and see if it would move, and thus really find out. They went to it, and three of them together used their greatest efforts to move it.

"Nanahboozhoo had to make one of the hardest efforts of his life to hold firm. However, he succeeded, and so the lions only said:

"'It really is a stump of a tree, but it is very strange we did not notice it before.' Then they rolled about on the warm sand in the sunshine until one after another fell asleep.

"Nanahboozhoo now noiselessly and quickly turned himself into a young hunter, then taking up his bow and arrow he shot the white lion. His arrow stuck fast in his body and badly wounded him, but did not kill him. At once the lions all plunged into the river and disappeared. Nanahboozhoo was sorry that he did not get the lion's skin, indeed he was greatly vexed and annoyed to have to return to his wigwam without it. A day or two after, as he was walking in the woods, he met with a very old woman. She had a bundle of slippery elm bark, out of which poultices were made by the Indians for wounds and bruises, and also some roots for medicine.

"'Where are you going, nookoom (grandmother), and what are you going to do with the bark and roots?'

"'O' said she, 'you cannot imagine what trouble we are in, for Nanahboozhoo has shot and badly wounded one of our chiefs, and great efforts are going to be made to catch and kill him.'

"She also told him that she had been honored in being sent for to come and use all of her healing arts to try and restore the wounded chief to health again, and that now she was on her way to his abode to poultice him with the slippery elm bark, and to give him medicine, made by boiling the roots, to allay the great fever from which he was suffering.

"Nanahboozhoo thus discovered that these lions, as he had supposed them to be, were wicked magicians who had been doing a great deal of harm, and who when they chose to do so could change themselves into the form of lions and live either under the water or on land, as best suited them, to escape from being killed by those whom they had injured. As the old woman was very talkative, Nanahboozhoo soon obtained from her all the information he desired. Among other things she told him that sometimes people came to her for bad medicines, to give to persons with whom they had quarreled, and in this way they would kill them with the poisons which she made out of toadstools and other deadly things.

"Hearing these dreadful facts from her own lips Nanahboozhoo resolved to kill her, but first he had her tell him where the wounded chief's abode was, and all about what was expected of her when she arrived there. He then speedily tomahawked her, and clothing himself in her garments he made himself look exactly like her, after which he took up her bundle of bark and roots and went to the dwelling of the chiefs.

"There he found quite a crowd assembled, but all were in confusion and excitement on account of the wounded chief. When they saw, as they thought, the old woman coming, whom they were eagerly expecting, they made way for her.

Nanahboozhoo went straight to the place where the wounded chief lay.

"He was surprised to see that the arrow which he had shot was still sticking in his side. He made a great ado about preparing the poultices and medicine, and set everybody around him doing something to help carry out his plans. Then when all were hurrying, and none looking at him, Nanahboozhoo pushed the arrow with such force into the body of the chief that it killed him instantly. Then with a shout of triumph he made his escape.

"There was, of course, great excitement among the people. They at once called a council and consulted what they should do to destroy Nanahboozhoo. They were, as I have told you, magicians, and had power to raise the waters, and so they resolved to drown him. They accordingly called on the waters to rise and rush over the plains and forests in the direction in which he lived. Nanahboozhoo had traveled with great speed back to his wigwam, but hardly had he reached it ere he heard the roar of the floods of water that were coming to overwhelm him. He saw his great danger and he ran away west, to the great mountains; but the floods of water continued rising and drove him up higher and higher. When he saw that he was nearing the highest peak he began to think what he must do next. Around him in the raging waters were quantities of logs and trees, and among them, or on the now small peak of land, were numbers of various animals.

"With all his powers he set to work and it was not very long ere he had a large raft made out of the floating logs. As the last spot of land was now being overwhelmed by the flood, and he pitied the animals that were swimming about, he took them on the raft with him. As Nanahboozhoo knew all the animals and their languages he held a council on the raft. He told them that if he could get even a very little of the old world that was drowned he could make a new world for them all. He first asked the otter if he would try, and see if he could dive down and bring up a little portion of the earth. The otter at once made the attempt, but after a while he came up to the surface apparently quite dead. Nanahboozhoo reached out and lifted him in and placed him in a sunny spot on the raft. Then the beaver tried. He took a great header and down he dived, resolved to succeed if possible, but after a time even he came up apparently as lifeless as the otter. Nanahboozhoo lifted his body up out of the water and laid it in the sun by the side of the otter. The muskrat next volunteered to try what he could do, so down he dived and, after a much longer time than the others had been down, he too floated up senseless and cold. Nanahboozhoo took him up, and as he did so he noticed that there was earth in his mouth and on his paws. He carefully collected this in his hand, and then placed the body of the muskrat beside the otter and the beaver. He then blew upon the earth and thus made it dry and porous, so that when it was placed in the water it would not sink but float. He then put a lively little mouse upon it, which by running round and round upon the earth made it grow larger and larger. Nanahboozhoo then put a squirrel upon it for the same object. Then the marten and mink--for the new earth was now so extended that it could hold up these light animals.

"For a time Nanahboozhoo had to guard the now rapidly growing young world from the larger animals with a stick, for fear they would sink it. They were all very tired of having to remain huddled together so long on the raft, and were eager to follow the smaller creatures that seemed so happy on the new earth, even if it were not very large as yet. As there was much to be done to fit this new world up for them to dwell upon, everyone had to do what he could. The birds were sent to fly over the water to pick up branches and seeds.

"By and by Nanahboozhoo decided that the earth, which had now grown beyond the reach of his eyes, was large enough, and so he revived the otter, the beaver and the muskrat, and with them and all the other animals around him he took possession of the new world.

"In order to ascertain the size of the world he sent a wolf to run to the end of it and then to return at once to him. The wolf easily made the journey in one day. Nanahboozhoo then kept him with him for some time, and again sent him off. The second journey took him five days, the third ten, the fourth a month, then he was gone a year and then five years. Thus it went on, until at length Nanahboozhoo started off a young wolf just able to run on the long journey. This one died of old age ere he had completed the trip. Nanahboozhoo then said that the world was large enough, and commanded it to cease from growing."

CHAPTER XIX.

Among the Briers and Wild Roses--Why the Roses have Thorns--Why the Wild Rabbits are White in Winter.

One day as the children were out in the clearings back of their home, gathering some of the wild strawberries that grew there and also some of the wildflowers that bloomed during the short brilliant summer, they were delighted to see Souwanas coming along the road with his gun on his shoulder and some ducks and rabbits in his hand.

Very cordial were their greetings, but soon the quick eyes of the kindly Indian noticed that there were several long red scratches and even some drops of partly dried blood on the hands of his little friends. It was hardly necessary for him to ask the cause of the wounds, as the bunches of sweet briers and wild roses, with their sharp needle-like thorns, in the happy children's hands told the tale.

Putting down his gun and game, Souwanas quickly gathered some of the sweet fragrant grass which is there so abundant, and skillfully twisting it into little coils he wound one around each of the bunches of flowers which the children had gathered, and which they were still having trouble to hold on account of the thorns.

The bouquets thus arranged could now be carried without inflicting any more wounds or pain. Amid their chat and laughter, for these white children were taught, like Indian children, not to be afraid of a few scratches or a little pain, Minnehaha, who was industriously wiping the blood from some wounds on her little white hands with her apron, said:

"How is it, Souwanas, that all these rosebushes and briers have such sharp thorns on them?"

"I suppose Mary would say that Nanahboozhoo, the rascal, had something to do with it," put in Sagastao.

At this reference to Mary there was a mischievous twinkle in the eyes of the old Indian.

"Yes," he replied, "Nanahboozhoo had lots to do with it, and yet when you hear the story you will see that he was not such a rascal at the time he did it as Mary would make out, but almost as good as her pet, Wakonda, who gave the bees their stings."

"O tell us all about it now," said Minnehaha. "We have this forenoon as a half holiday, and papa is to join us in about an hour for a walk in the woods."

The kind-hearted old Indian had been pleased with the plucky way in which the children had slighted their wounded hands, and before he began his story he acted the part of the skillful physician. He found some soft juicy leaves which he crushed and spread on the ugly red scratches. The effect was magical, and the children who had so bravely treated their wounds with indifference gratefully acknowledged the sudden cessation of the smart.

Selecting a pretty spot under a clump of balsam trees, where some boulder-like stones afforded them comfortable seats, the children cuddled down with their old friend, to hear how the roses got their thorns.

"Long ago the roses were the most abundant of flowers, but they grew on bushes that were smooth and fragrant, and such delicious eating that all the animals that eat grass or browse were constantly seeking for and devouring not only the rose flowers but also the bushes on which they grew. The result was that the roses of all kinds were in danger of being exterminated. In those days trees and flowers and other things had greater powers of thinking and acting than they have now, and so the roses of different kinds met in council to decide what could be done to preserve those of them that were still left in existence. It was decided that a deputation of them should be sent to Nanahboozhoo to implore his assistance.

"He is such an eccentric fellow, and assumes so many disguises, that they had a good deal of difficulty in finding him. They traveled long distances, and inquired of the various wild animals they met and even consulted the trees and hills. At length they were informed that he was now living in a valley among the mountains and experimenting as a gardener. They hurried away as fast as the fierce wind which they had hired to carry them could blow them along. At first when they reached his abode they were very much frightened, as it was easy to observe from the loud angry tones in which Nanahboozhoo, although afar off, was speaking, that he was in a great rage. However, they had come too far to be easily discouraged. They quietly drew near, and hiding behind some dense balsam trees they carefully listened to find out the cause of his anger. Fortunately, they could not have come at a better time for themselves, for it seems that Nanahboozhoo had become very much interested in his work as a gardener. All the things he had planted had grown so well that in order to protect them from prowling wild animals he had set all around the garden a fine hedge of rosebushes. So many were required that Nanahboozhoo had been obliged to transplant bushes from a great distance around, for they did not grow so abundantly as formerly.

"The morning of the very day on which the deputation of the rosebushes arrived Nanahboozhoo had returned from one of his short adventures. Fancy his indignation at finding that in his absence all sorts of animals, from the rabbit to the mountain elk, had visited his abode, and had not only completely eaten that lovely hedge of rosebushes, but had also greatly injured the beautiful garden, of which he was so proud!

"When the deputation of roses understood the cause of his wrath they at once left their hiding places and, aided by a sudden puff of wind, came before Nanahboozhoo. The sight of them excited his curiosity, as it had seemed to him that every rosebush had been destroyed. Before he could say a word, however, the rosebushes, who were then able to talk, at once presented their petition and pleaded for his powerful assistance to save them from being exterminated by their enemies.

"Nanahboozhoo listened to their petition, and after some consultation with the rose bushes it was decided to cover the stocks and branches, up to the very beautiful flowers, with small thorn-like prickles, so that every animal henceforth would be afraid to either devour or closely approach them, as they had been accustomed to do in the past. With this protection granted them they were more than pleased, and so it now happens that roses of many kinds still exist in various parts of the world."

"Thank you very much for that story," said Minnehaha. "Even if Nanahboozhoo did put prickles on the rosebushes he was not a rascal, for we would not have had any roses at all but for what he did."

For a wonder, Sagastao was silent for a time; but at length he found something to say, and his words were a bit of a confession and promise of amendment:

"Now that I know why it is that the prickles are on the wild roses I'll not get mad even if my fingers bleed when I am gathering a bouquet for mother."

At this moment the two favorite dogs, Jack and Cuffy, came bounding up. By this the children knew that their father was not far behind, and they were not disappointed. At first he looked anxious when he saw the little hands wrapped up in green leaves, but as with merry laughs they told him what the leaves were for everything was bright again.

Souwanas was greeted very cordially, as usual, and assured that at the mission house he would find in the mistress a willing purchaser of his ducks and rabbits. The children were always interested in the game, although Minnehaha strongly declared that it was a pity to kill the pretty creatures. Souwanas and their father were chatting together while the children were turning the ducks and rabbits over.

"See what red eyes some of the ducks have," said Sagastao. "They look as though they had been crying."

"Guess you would have cried too," rather indignantly replied Minnehaha, "if you had been shot as they were."

"Huh!" he replied with a tinge of contempt, "how could they cry after being shot? I don't believe that is it at all. And, look here, Minnehaha, I am going also to ask why it is that, while all the rabbits were so white in winter, they are all now so brown in summer."

Quickly the resolve was carried out, and so, while Minnehaha was telling her father what a beautiful story they had heard about the roses, Sagastao, with his hand on the shoulder of the old Indian, who was seated on a rock, was eagerly firing at him his double-barreled question: "Why have some ducks such red eyes, and why are the rabbits white in winter and brown in summer?"

"Both done by Nanahboozhoo," said the old man with a smile, as he took his pipe out of his mouth.

"Hurrah for Nanahboozhoo!" shouted the lad.

This outburst on the part of Sagastao at once attracted the attention of the others to him and Minnehaha wanted to know what was the matter now.

"Why, did you not hear? Souwanas says that Nanahboozhoo gave the ducks the red eyes and makes the rabbits to be white in winter and brown in summer." Then turning to Souwanas he asked, "How does Nanahboozhoo do it?"

Here the father, while amused at the lad's enthusiasm, interposed, and said:

"You have already kept Souwanas a long time, and perhaps he is busy."

"Busy!" said the irrepressible Sagastao, who was shrewd beyond his years. "Busy! Why Souwanas would rather tell stories than do anything else--unless to smoke his pipe."

Then he glibly told Souwanas in Saulteaux what had passed between him and his father in English, and added, "Is that not so, Souwanas?"

The old Indian smiled, and said kindly:

"How can I help enjoying telling stories when I have such good little listeners?"

"But what about his dinner?" asked the kind-hearted Minnehaha. "If we keep him here telling stories he will be too late to get back to his wigwam for his dinner. I think we had better take him home with us."

This was quickly decided upon, and that there might be no mistake a piece of bark was quickly cut from a birch tree and a few lines written upon it telling the good mother in the home that they had met Souwanas, and that he was entertaining the children with Nanahboozhoo stories and would be with them to dinner. Then Jack, the great dog, was called and sent back with the missive, with orders to give it to his mistress.

As the dog dashed away homeward the mischievous Sagastao said:

"My! don't I wish I was in the kitchen when Mary hears that we are out here with Souwanas listening to stories about Nanahboozhoo! Won't she be hopping mad!"

"It will be better," said his father, "for Souwanas to tell his story than for you to make any further remarks of that kind."

At first Souwanas seemed to show some hesitancy in beginning his story in the presence of his missionary, and he whispered to Sagastao his fears that perhaps his father would not care for such trifles as Indian legends and stories.

With his usual bluntness, the lad declared:

"O, you don't know our father if you think that way about him. He loves nice stories as well as we do, and tells us lots of them; so go ahead, for you are going home to dinner with us."

Thus assured, the old man began:

"I will tell you to-day about how it is that the rabbits are white in winter.

"Long ago they were always brown, just like those that are lying there with the ducks. It is true that they increase very fast, but then it is very true that they have many enemies. They have not many ways to defend themselves against their foes, who are of so many kinds. Almost all the animals that live on flesh are always hunting for rabbits, and so are the foxes of all kinds, the wild cats, wolves, and wolverines, and even the little weasels and ermine. Then there are fierce birds--the eagle, the hawks of all kinds and the owls--that are always on the lookout for rabbits, young or old.

"The result was that with this war continually being waged against them the poor rabbits had a hard time of it, and especially in winter; for they found it very difficult to hide themselves when the leaves were off the trees and the ground covered with snow. In those days in the long ago the animals used to have a great council. There the great fathers or heads of each kind of animal and bird used to meet together and talk about their welfare and the welfare of each other. Then there was peace and friendship among them while at the council.

"They appointed a king, and he presided as a great head chief. All the animals that had troubles or grievances had a right to come and speak about them and, if possible, have them remedied.

"Some queer things were said sometimes. At one council the bear found great fault with the fox, who had deceived him, and had caused him to lose his beautiful tail by telling him to go and catch fish in a big crack in the ice. He sat there so long that the crack froze up solidly and to save his life he had to break off his tail.

"But all the things they talked about were not so funny as that. They had their troubles and dangers, and they discussed various plans for improving their condition and considered how they could best defeat the skill and cleverness of the human hunters.

"When the rabbit's turn came to be heard he had indeed a sorrowful tale to tell. He said that his people were nearly all destroyed. The rest of the world seemed combined against his race, and they were killing them by day and night, in summer and winter, and they had but little power to fight against their many enemies. They were almost discouraged, but had come to the council to see if their brethren could suggest any remedy or plan to save them from complete destruction. While the rabbit was speaking the wolverine winked at the wildcat, while the fox, although he tried to look solemn, could not keep his mouth from watering at the thought of the many rabbits he intended yet to eat.

"Thus it can be seen that the poor, harmless rabbit did not get much sympathy from that part of the crowd that killed his race all the rest of the year.

"Still there were some animals, like the moose, and the reindeer, and the mountain goat, that stood up in the council and spoke out bravely for the rabbit. Indeed they told the animals that had only laughed at the rabbit's sad story that, if nothing was done for the little rabbit and they went on killing as they were doing, they would soon be the greatest sufferers, for if the rabbits were all gone there was nothing else that they could get in sufficient numbers to keep them alive. This, which is a fact, rather sobered some of them at first; but they soon resumed their mocking at the poor little rabbit and his story, and, as they were in the majority, the council refused to do anything in the matter.

"When the moose heard the decision of the council he was very sorry for his poor little brother the rabbit, so after thinking it over he told the rabbit to jump up on one of his flat horns while he was holding them down. Then the moose carried him out some distance from the council meeting, and said:

"There is no hope for you here. The most of the animals live on you, and so they will not do anything that will make it more difficult for you to be caught than it is now. Your only chance is to go to Nanahboozhoo, and see what he can do for you."

"Hurrah!" shouted Sagastao. "I thought it would be to Nanahboozhoo after all."

Continuing, Souwanas said:

"The moose encouraged the rabbit by saying, 'Nanahboozhoo's name was once Manabush, or Keche-Wapoose, Great Rabbit, and so I am sure he will be your friend, as I think he is a distant relation.'

"Not waiting for the council to close, away sped the rabbit along the route described by the moose, who had lately found out where Nanahboozhoo was stopping. The rabbit was such a timid creature that when he came near to Nanahboozhoo he was much afraid that he would not be welcomed. However, his case was desperate, and although his heart was thumping within him with fear he hurried along to have the thing over as soon as possible. To his great joy he found Nanahboozhoo in the best of humor and he was received most kindly.

"Nanahboozhoo saw how wearied and tired the rabbit was after the long journey, and so he made him rest on some fragrant grass in the sunshine while he went out and brought in for him to eat some of the choicest things from his garden. Then afterward he had the rabbit tell of all his troubles and of how he was treated at the council.

"This part of the story, of how they acted at the council, made Nanahboozhoo very angry.

"'And that's the way they treated this little brother at the council we have given them, where it is expected that the smallest and the weakest shall have the same right to have his case heard and attended to as the biggest and strongest! It is high time that somebody was coming to me with council news if things are like this. Look out, Mister Fox, and Wolverine, and Wild Cat, for if I get after you I will so straighten you out that you will be sorry that the rabbit had to go to Nanahboozhoo for the help you ought to have given him!'

"Nanahboozhoo had worked himself up into such a furious temper that the rabbit was almost frightened to death. But when he saw this Nanahboozhoo only laughed at him, and said he was sorry to have scared him.

"'I was so angry,' said Nanahboozhoo, 'at those animals for ill-treating you that I forgot myself; and now, little brother, what do you want me to do for you?'

"They had a long talk about the matter and the decision was that there should be two great changes. The first was that the eyes of the rabbit were to be so increased in power that they should in future be able to see by night as well as by day, and the second was that in all Northlands where much snow falls during many months of the year rabbits shall change into a beautiful white color, like the snow, and thus continue as long as the winter lasts. And the rabbits now have a much better time than they had formerly. They can glide away in the darkness from their enemies when in the woods, and when out in the snow they are not easily seen and often escape notice by remaining perfectly still."

But long ere Souwanas had ended Jack had returned from the home with a note to say that dinner would soon be ready, and that no one could be more welcome than Souwanas.

"But what about the red eyes of the ducks?" said the two children, whose appetites for stories were simply--well, like those of other boys and girls.

Here the father had to interfere and say that there had been quite enough for one day. However, before the walk homeward began, Souwanas was pledged to tell the other story at the first convenient opportunity.

CHAPTER XX.

Passing Hunters and Their Spoils--The Vain Woman--Why the Marten has
a White Spot on His Breast.

As the home where Sagastao and Minnehaha lived was near a trail along
which numbers of Indian hunters were accustomed to travel when on
their way to the trading post with their furs, they frequently called in
to see their loved friends the palefaces. These hunters were always welcome, and as they were very seldom in a hurry the children drew from them many
a quaint Indian legend or story of animal life.

It was also a great pleasure for the children to have the hunters, returning
from a successful trip, open their fur packs and spread out before them the rich furs
and tell them stories about these animals--the silver fox, the otter, beavers, minks,
martens, ermines, and sometimes even about great bears and wolves, whose skin
they had often had. These valuable furs were generally well dressed and prepared
for shipment by the industrious women before they were taken to the trading post.
Sometimes, however, a hunter when on the trail to the trading post would find in
one of his traps an animal just caught, and not having time to return to his wigwam
and have the skin dressed and dried he would carry the animal just as it was and sell
it to the fur traders.

One day there called a number of Indians, and among them was a hunter with
a couple of martens which he had caught in his trap that very morning. Sagastao
and Minnehaha had never seen these little animals before, and they handled them
with much interest and asked several questions about them.

"Why has the marten that queer white spot on its throat?" asked Minnehaha.

The Indians looked at each other and a grim smile flitted over their bronzed faces when they heard this question.

Their conduct only the more excited the curiosity of the children and they both clamored for the answer. Then one of the Indians said:

"Ask Mary; she knows all about the story, and as a woman was in the affair she can tell it better than we can."

With this answer the children had to be content, for the hunters, having drank their cups of tea, soon took their departure.

When the children found Mary they at once demanded the story.

"What story?" said Mary.

"O, you know what we want, for you were in the kitchen and heard what was said."

But Mary still protested her ignorance, and declared that she had been so busy caring for Souwanaquenapeke that she had not listened to half the chatter that had passed between them and the Indians.

"O, I know you, sakehow Mary," said Sagastao. "You don't want to tell us because there was a woman like yourself mixed up in it."

Mary bridled up with indignation, but before she could utter a word the arms of Sagastao were around her neck, and he cried:

"Forgive me, sakehou! for speaking so foolishly. I do remember now that you had left the kitchen with baby before Minnehaha asked the question."

This prompt apology and the sweet word "sakehow" restored harmony, and Mary was now anxious to please them.

"What was the question which interested you?" asked Mary.

"Why has the marten that queer white spot on its throat?" asked Minnehaha.

"And the men told us to go to you because there was a woman in it," added Sagastao.

Mary smiled when she heard this.

"Yes," she said, "there was a foolish woman mixed up in the story. It was like this, as far as I can remember, and it is a story from the North people. Long ago a man had a wife who was a very proud, vain woman. She was not contented with having her husband and her own people saying nice things about her, but she wanted to be flattered and admired by every creature. You know that I have told you that, in old times, animals could talk and do many things. Well, this conceited woman, with her silly foolish way, began attracting the different animals around her. Almost everybody was laughing at her, but she seemed to think it great fun to have so many admirers. She got a lesson one day when flirting with the bear. They were walking along together and she let him put his arm around her, but he gave her such a hug that he broke two of her ribs. She was a long time getting well and then her husband gave her a great lecturing. You would have thought that this would have cured her, but not a bit of it. When she was well again she was just as silly as ever, though she took good care not to flirt with any animal that could hug like a bear. She next bewitched the skunk with her foolishness. But one day, as they walked together, a dog suddenly attacked the skunk and in his anger and excitement he so perfumed the woman, instead of the dog, with his odor that her husband found her out and gave her a beating.

"Everybody was now laughing at her on account of her silly ways, and as her husband had persons employed to see what creatures she went out walking with she had to remain at home in her wigwam. But when a woman gets proud and conceited and carries on like this one did she is hard to cure. The fact was, her husband was too kind to her. He did not give her plenty of work to keep her busy and out of mischief. Instead of making her chop the wood and carry the water, and do other hard things, he did it for her, for he was very proud of her and she was indeed a beautiful woman. He did, however, make her stay in their wigwam instead of allowing her to go about wherever she liked.

"She spent most of her time in fixing herself up in her beautiful clothes and thinking what a lovely creature she was. But she soon missed the flattery of her admirers and resolved that, in spite of her husband, she would try to hear it again. So vigilant, however, were her husband and his friends that they were too clever for her.

"One day her husband returned from hunting and visiting his traps and snares. Among other animals that he had trapped was a beautiful marten. He had caught it in what is called a dead-fall; that is, where a log is so arranged that when the animal reaches the bait he is directly under the log, which falls upon him the instant he pulls the bait.

"When the woman took up the marten which her husband had thrown at her feet she noticed that it was still quite warm, but she said nothing about it to her husband, who, picking up an ax and blanket, said that he was going off to visit his more distant traps and would not be back for some days. Before he left he made her promise that she would not leave the wigwam until his return.

"The woman, as soon as she was sure that her husband was really gone, picked up the marten. On examining it she was convinced that it was not dead, only knocked senseless by the falling log, so she rubbed it, and breathed into its nostrils, and then with a reed blew air into its lungs.

"Sure enough, the life was in it, and the first sign it gave was a big sneeze or two. At this the woman wrapped it up in a warm covering and held it until it was well again. The marten, of course, was very much frightened when it found itself in the hands of a woman. It was about to struggle to get free, when the woman spoke to it in its own language. At this it was very much surprised, and more so when the woman told it how she had given it back its life, and that now in return it must do what she desired.

"Any animal or human being would be willing to promise as much when its life had been thus restored to it.

"'I will do anything I can for you,' said the marten.

"'I want you to go to your king marten,' said the woman, 'and tell him that a beautiful lady has heard so many wonderful things about him that she is very anxious to have a visit from him.'

"This the marten promised to do, and it was not very long before the king marten came. Of course he had to be very cautious, as he had been warned of the many who were watching the silly woman.

"Hardly, however, had he time to say much to her before the footsteps of her husband were heard outside. The instant he opened the door of the wigwam the king marten ran out, and disappeared in the forest.

"'What was that?' asked the husband.

"'O, dear, that was the marten you trapped. It must have come to life and escaped,' said the woman, who thus cleverly saved herself and the king marten.

"The man was suspicious, but as the marten which he had trapped was not to be found he could not find fault with her, except to say that she ought to have skinned the marten soon after he had brought it in.

"The king marten, who was a very conceited fellow, had been quite struck with the beauty of the woman, and so, in spite of his narrow escape, he resolved to go and see her again. By watching her husband's departure he managed to have several brief visits, and at length became so infatuated with her that he tried to coax her to run away with him.

"When she heard this she was very angry, for, with all her foolishness, she had only acted as she did because of her vanity and love of flattery. Now that the marten had dared make such a request she resolved that he should be punished; so one day, when he was sitting beside her and saying a lot of foolish flattery, she heard the footsteps of her husband approaching, but did not warn the king marten.

"So the man thus caught the old marten sitting by the side of his wife. At this he was much annoyed, and as the marten suddenly ran out the man asked the woman what it meant. So she told him all that the marten had said, and of his impertinence in asking her to leave him and become the marten's wife. At this the man was very indignant, and so they arranged to punish the marten.

"The next time the man went off he told his wife to fill the kettle with water and put it on the fire to boil. Then the man took his traps and started off as though he were going on a long journey. But he only went a little way, just far enough to throw the marten off his guard, and, sure enough, while he was watching he saw the marten go into the wigwam.

"Then the man came quietly to the door and listened. He heard the marten urging his wife to leave and run away with him. Then he suddenly sprang into the tent and shouted out:

"'Old king marten, what are you doing here? How dare you talk to my wife?'

"So saying, the man seized the kettle of boiling water and threw its contents at the marten, severely scalding him. The marten tore at his burning breast as he dashed away into the woods. And from that day to this all martens have that whitish spot on their chests caused by that burn."

"What became of the woman?" said Sagastao.

"Never mind now. We have wasted too much time already on such a good-for-nothing conceited flirt," said Mary.

CHAPTER XXI.

Shooting Loons--Why the Loon has a Flat Back, Red Eyes, and Such Queer Feet--Nanahboozhoo Loses His Dinner--Origin of Lichens--Why Some Willows are Red--The Partridge.

Nothing gave the children greater pleasure than to have the Indians take them in their canoes for a couple of hours' trip on the bright waters of the beautiful lake that spread out before their home.

These pleasant outings were sometimes rendered exciting and doubly interesting by the sight of a black bear or a deer wandering on the shore or swimming from some point on the island. At other times there would be numbers of loons, or great Northern divers, as they are generally called. Their wonderful quickness in diving, then the length of time that they could remain under the water and the great distance they would swim before coming to the surface were watched with great interest by both Sagastao and Minnehaha.

The Indians did not often hunt loons. In fact they found it so difficult to shoot one that more than its value in ammunition was generally expended in the attempt. The Indians always declared that these clever birds could see the flash of their guns and dive down out of danger before the shot reached them.

However, as some of them were desired for their beautiful feather-covered skins, which make most valuable and beautiful caps and muffs, it was decided that Souwanas and Kennedy should take the missionary's breech-loading rifle, in addition to their own guns, and try to secure a few.

The children begged to be allowed to accompany them, and as the day was unusually fine and the lake almost without a ripple they were given a holiday and allowed the privilege of an all-day outing with these two trusty and experienced men.

A generous lunch, with the indispensable tea kettle, was placed in the canoe by careful Mary, who, as usual, was angry that the children were to be so long under the witchery of old Souwanas.

With the merry shouts of laughter from the children as their accompaniment the two Indians skillfully plied their paddles, and it was not long before they were some miles distant and on the lookout for loons. It often happens that the things desired are the last to come. So it was this day. Wild ducks in goodly numbers, and even geese and some swans and pelicans were frequently seen. At length, however, strange, mournful sounds far ahead were heard, and the experienced Indians knew that the birds for which they were looking were not far away. Still it was some time before the first long white neck and black head were seen in the distance, for the cry of the loon not only differs from that of any other bird, but is very far-reaching.

The excited children were now told to be very still and keep quiet, using their eyes alone, and witness the contest between man's skill and the birds' cleverness.

So accustomed have some old loons become to being fired at and missed by Indians using the old-fashioned flintlock shotgun, which makes such a flash when fired, that they just barely keep out of range. The instant they see the fire flash-- down they go, and then as the shot or bullet strikes the place where they were they bob up again serenely in the same spot, or in one not very far distant. This risky sport some of them will keep up for hours, or until the disheartened hunters have wasted nearly all their ammunition.

To-day, however, there was to be a new weapon tried against them, and, alas for them, they were sadly worsted. Kennedy first loaded his old flintlock shotgun and blazed away, but, as usual, they were out of sight under the water before the shot struck the place where the loons had been.

For a time the loons were shy, and swam quite a distance away. But after a while, as they found that Kennedy's gunshots could be dodged, they did not bother to swim very far away. This was just what Souwanas was waiting for. He now took up the rifle, and as soon as a loon came to the surface he fired from this new weapon, that gave no flash to warn the poor bird of the deadly bullet that was so rapidly speeding on its way. Thus it happened that loon after loon was struck and several beautiful birds were secured--greatly to the sorrow of the children, who delighted in watching their clever diving and sudden reappearance after Kennedy discharged his old gun. Out of deference to their feelings the Indians soon ceased shooting, although with this new rifle they could easily have secured many more.

"Let us now go ashore, on one of these islands," said Sagastao, "and have our lunch."

"And a Nanahboozhoo story after," put in Minnehaha.

This plan was just what the Indians were thinking about, and so in a short time they were all on the shore. Dry wood was abundant and a bright fire was soon burning, and then, when the water was boiled and the tea made, the lunch basket was opened and the meal was much enjoyed by all.

"Now, Souwanas," said Minnehaha, "we are all ready for the story at the same time, and if your pipe goes out I'll hand you a burning stick with which you can light it again."

"Maybe I will keep you very busy," remarked the old man, much amused at the offer--and so it proved, for his pipe to-day persisted in going out.

"One day," began Souwanas, "as Nanahboozhoo was walking along the shore of a lake he became hungry. He considered what it would be best for him to do in order to procure something to eat. He decided to deceive the waterfowls. He saw a duck swimming along near the shore and spoke to the bird in this fashion:

"'Come here, my brother.'

"'What is it?' said the duck, as it approached Nanahboozhoo.

"'Kesha Munedoo (Gracious Spirit) has revealed words to me to tell to all the waterfowl some very important things. Go and tell all sorts of waterfowl to come, and when they are all together I will inform you what has been revealed to me.'

"The duck obeyed Nanahboozhoo, who in the meantime made a very bare wigwam of green boughs, or rather caused it to appear that he did, for he did not exert much labor upon it. All sorts of waterfowl came to Nanahboozhoo and they seemed anxious to hear what had been revealed. Nanahboozhoo received them with great apparent friendliness and invited them to come into the wigwam. When they had all entered, he said:

"'You must all dance, first, before I tell you what has been revealed to me. All of you must stand close together around inside of the wigwam and put your necks close together while dancing, and all of you must flap your wings at the same time.'

"Then Nanahboozhoo commenced singing:

"'Pau-zau-gwa-be-she-moog,   Ke-ku-ma-mis-kwa-she-gun.'

("'Shut your eyes,   And I'll make you wise.')

"These words Nanahboozhoo repeated three times.

"All the fowl kept time to the music and words of the song, and danced, shutting their eyes. Nanahboozhoo continued singing, changing to the following words:

"'Au-yun-ze-kwa-gau.'

"All the time such was Nanahboozhoo's power over the birds that they kept singing and dancing and at the same time holding their heads close together. Nanahboozhoo's voice was singing in the center of the tent, his drum beating at the same time, while he in person went around in the wigwam or lodge wringing the necks of the waterfowl and throwing them on the side of the lodge. The loon, the great diver bird, was dancing on the open door side of the lodge. He suspected that Nanahboozhoo was up to some of his tricks, doing something bad, so he opened his eyes and saw. At once he gave the alarm, and shouted:

"'Nanahboozhoo is killing us!'

"All the fowl that were still alive when they heard these words at once flew out at the top opening of the lodge, except the loon, or diver, and he being at the door turned and ran out of the lodge as fast as he could toward the shore of the lake.

"Nanahboozhoo was so angry at him for daring to open his eyes, and then for warning the others, enabling many of them to get away, that he ran after him and stamped upon him as he had just reached the shore. Hence it is, because of Nanahboozhoo's cruelty, that the loon has had a flat back and red eyes, and its feet are so unlike those of any other waterfowl.

"When Nanahboozhoo had made a large fire he took the waterfowls he had killed before the diver gave the alarm, and covered them under the ashes, leaving only their feet sticking out. While he was waiting for them to cook he felt very sleepy, so he lay down to rest.

"But before he went to sleep he said, 'My face side has always done all the watching. This is not fair. I will make my back do its share of the watching.'

"So, as he cuddled down to have a sleep before the fire, he said to his back:

"'Now, you do the watching, you lazy, broad back, while I am sleeping.' Then, being very tired, he fell into a heavy sleep.

"After a time the watcher called out:

"'Nanahboozhoo! Indians are coming!'

"Nanahboozhoo slightly raised himself, but he saw no Indians, so he lay down to sleep again.

"But again and yet again, for three times, did his faithful watcher call and warn him against his approaching enemies. Nanahboozhoo was now so stupid with sleep that he only aroused himself a little, not enough to enable him to detect the lurking enemy. So he became very angry with his watcher, his broad back, and gave it a great thrashing, saying:

"'There! take that, you great stupid watcher, for so disturbing me with your false reports!'

"Then Nanahboozhoo fell asleep again. The broad back was very much offended at the treatment he had received, for he knew he was right, and now, though the Indians were close at hand, he did not again warn Nanahboozhoo, so the enemies came and stole all of his cooked fowls. The Indians carefully lifted out the fowls by their legs, which Nanahboozhoo left sticking up. When they had eaten the bodies of the fowls they stuck back the legs in the ashes, as Nanahboozhoo had left them.

"When at last his sleep was ended Nanahboozhoo arose ready for his meal of nicely cooked fowl. Great, indeed, were his surprise and indignation when he pulled out the feet from the ashes and found that the bodies of the fowls were not there.

"He flew into a passion and resolved to punish his back. So he made a fire of big trees and stood with his back very close to it. When his flesh began to be badly burned it blistered, and made a noise like the roasting of meat. Nanahboozhoo did not at first seem to mind the pain, and only said:

"'You may well say 'Zeeng, Zeeng,' in your burning. I will teach you a lesson you will remember for not telling me that the Indians were stealing my roasted waterfowl.'

"Nanahboozhoo then went on his way, but in spite of his magic powers he felt a sort of a soreness in his back. He twisted his head around and saw the blisters that had been made by the fierce fire. So he thought how he must get rid of them, for they bothered him, although nothing could injure him for very long. While walking on the edge of a precipice he slipped--and away he slid, far down the rocky side.

When he reached the bottom, he looked back, and there, on the rock, on which he had slid down, he saw things which he had never seen before.

"'My nephews,' said Nanahboozhoo, 'when they see these things on the rocks, will call them Wau-konug (lichen), and although they are poor food they will keep them from starving when they have nothing better.'

"This is the Indian tradition of the origin of the patches of lichen attached to the bare rocks. The Indians still call them 'no-scabs,' and when boiled they make a kind of jelly food which is a little better than starvation.

"Then Nanahboozhoo, although his back was bleeding from his sliding down the rough rocks, continued walking, sometimes along the shore and sometimes in the thick bush. In one place where the thicket was very dense such was his magic power that he pulled a lot of the thickets together and walked over on their tops. When he looked back he saw that the blood from the wounds in his back had given a red color to the bushes over which he had walked. Then said Nanahboozhoo:

"'My nephews will call these bushes "Me-squah-be-me-sheen" (red willows). They will use them to stop bleeding when they meet with any severe accidents;' and such the Indians still do when they live among them.

"This is the tradition as to the origin of the red willow, once so common in many of the Indian haunts.

"The reason why the partridge is called Kosh-ko-e-wa-soo (one that startles) is because one made even Nanahboozhoo give a big jump. It happened in this way:

"As Nanahboozhoo was walking along one day in the woods he saw a small creature. This little thing thought it would be best for him to be brave in the presence of Nanahboozhoo, and so when he was asked who he was he answered:

"'I am one who startles.'

"'You cannot startle me,' said Nanahboozhoo.

"The little creature suddenly flew away and Nanahboozhoo resumed his journey. By and by he reached a dangerous rocky point on the shore. Just as he was at the worst point the partridge suddenly flew almost from under his feet with a rumbling noise, and so startled him that he jumped up, sprang quickly aside, fell into the water, and got a great wetting. So even Nanahboozhoo had to confirm the name of the little partridge."

The return trip was not much enjoyed by the children. The dead loons in the canoe did not look as attractive as they had appeared when swimming and diving so gracefully in the lake. Souwanas was quick to notice their depression of spirits, and he there and then resolved that he would never again shoot any living thing in their presence, and he faithfully kept his resolve.

Mary met them as they landed and her quick eyes detected the change in their spirits, and as they wore their hearts on their sleeves for her she quickly found out the cause of their sorrow. She was not slow in availing herself of the opportunity afforded of giving Souwanas and Kennedy a vigorous scolding for nearly breaking the hearts of her precious darlings, by killing in their presence some of the birds whose play they had often watched for hours together.

The two men took her scolding in their usual silent way, and then had a quiet laugh together when her wrath had exhausted itself and she had indignantly walked off with the children.

CHAPTER XXII.

Nanahboozhoo's Ride on the Back of the Buzzard, who Lets Him Fall--A
Short-lived Triumph--Why the Buzzard has No Feathers on His Head or
Neck.

One beautiful warm day, when the leaves of the trees were all bright and
golden with their autumnal tints, the children were visiting at the tent
of Souwanas.

The old man was making a beautiful little bow and a quiver full of arrows for Sagastao while the old wife was manufacturing an elaborate baby cradle,
of the Indian pattern, for Minnehaha, in which she could carry her favorite doll in
the style popular among the Indian girls.

The children were much interested in watching these highly-prized gifts being
prepared for them, and of course had much to say in the way of thanks to those who
were doing so much to add to their happiness.

While they were thus busy several canoes were seen coming from the south.
As the wind was favorable sails had been improvised out of blankets, each fastened
to a couple of oars, and with these simple appliances they sped rapidly along. Seeing
Souwanas's wigwam on the point of land the Indians came to the shore and smoked
and chatted for a short time ere they resumed their journey toward the north.

They had in their canoes quite a variety of game, and among them a large ill-
smelling bird called a turkey-buzzard. It was said that the young Indian hunter who
had shot it thought at first that it really was a turkey, but he found out his mistake
when he went to lift it from the ground where it had fallen. The odor was so of-
fensive that at first he thought he would leave it behind, but when he remembered
that often some of the large feathers were used in ornamental work he decided to
bring it along.

The children were interested in its appearance, as this was the first dead turkey-buzzard they had ever seen.

"Look, Souwanas," said Minnehaha, "the poor birdie has no feathers on its neck or head. It must be very cold there when the winter comes."

"Well, I think that, as likely as not, it was its own fault that it lost its feathers," said Sagastao, and then he added as he poked the rank bird over with a stick:

"I would not be surprised to hear that Nanahboozhoo had something to do with it."

"Nanahboozhoo had," said Souwanas, "and it was because of a mean trick that the buzzard played upon him. And now that these Indians are off, who are in a hurry to reach Poplar Point, if you will sit down on the rocks in the warm sunshine I will tell you the story."

No second invitation was necessary, so while the children seated themselves near him on the; smooth granite rock the old man continued his arrow making and told them the following story:

"One day when Nanahboozhoo was walking through the country he saw the buzzard soaring up high in the air. Like an eagle, he was making graceful circles round and round with very little effort. After a time the buzzard flew down to the earth, and there he stood on a rock with his great wings outstretched. Nanahboozhoo quietly approached and entered into conversation with him.

"'Brother Buzzard,' he said, 'you must be very happy when sailing around up there in the blue sky where you can so easily see everything that is going on down here on the world below you. I wish you would take me up there on your back and let me see how this world looks from that high place in the blue sky, where you live so much.'

"The buzzard on hearing this request at once flew down to the side of Nanahboozhoo and said:

"'I will with pleasure take you up on my back and let you see, as you desire, how the world looks from that high place.'

"Then Nanahboozhoo, seeing how smooth was the back of the great bird, said:

"'Brother Buzzard, your back is so smooth that I am afraid I will slip off, so you must be careful not to sweep round too rapidly in your circles in the sky.'

"The buzzard told Nanahboozhoo that he would be very careful although at the same time he was resolved, if it were possible, to play a trick on him; for he had a grudge of some long standing against him which Nanahboozhoo seemed to have forgotten.

"Nanahboozhoo then mounted on the back of the great buzzard and held by his feathers as well as he possibly could. The buzzard then took a short run, sprang from the ground, and spreading his great strong wings speedily rose up higher and higher in the sky.

"Nanahboozhoo at first felt rather timid as he found himself thus rapidly soaring through the air, especially as it was so difficult for him to keep his seat. When the buzzard began circling round and round it was even more difficult, for the body of the bird leaned over more and more as his speed increased. But Nanahboozhoo was very clever, and after a while he became more accustomed to his queer position and was very much interested in the splendid sights of the great world beneath him, over which he could now see for such a great distance. Lakes and rivers, forests and mountains, all gave delight to Nanahboozhoo, who had wonderful powers of vision.

"At length, as they rose up higher and higher in the blue sky, Nanahboozhoo shouted out in his delight as far away in the distance he recognized the wigwam of his grandmother, Nokomis. Indeed so delighted was he that for a moment he let go his hold on the buzzard and swung up his arms in his excitement. The treacherous buzzard noticed this, saw it was the opportunity for which he had been watching, and circled round so suddenly that his body was tilted over, and before Nanahboozhoo could regain his grip he slipped off the smooth back and fell like a stone to the ground. So terrible was the force with which he struck the earth that he was knocked senseless, and lay there for a long time like one dead.

"But, as I have told you, Nanahboozhoo was more than human and nothing could really kill him. So it happened that after a while he recovered his senses, but he was annoyed, disgusted, that he had allowed the buzzard to play such a mean trick on him.

"Then he prepared to resume his journey, and of course he looked up to see if there were any sign of the buzzard. He had not far to look, for there, up in the sky, not far off, was the old buzzard laughing at the trick he had played upon Nanahboozhoo, and much pleased with his own cleverness in deceiving one known to be so crafty.

"'Laugh away, old buzzard,' said Nanahboozhoo. 'You have had the best of me this time, but look out! For I will put a mark upon you for this trick of yours that will enable your friends and your enemies to recognize you both by day and by night.'

"But the buzzard, from his high safe place in the sky, only laughed back in derision, and said:

"'No, indeed, Nanahboozhoo, you will do nothing of the kind. You have been deceiving the other creatures, but in me you have found your match. You cannot deceive me. And now, especially as you have threatened me, I will always be on the watch for you.'

"Nanahboozhoo made no reply to this boastful speech, but he did a lot of thinking, and he soon had his plans laid to teach Mr. Buzzard a lesson he would never forget.

"Resuming his journey he pushed on as though nothing had happened.

"The buzzard was at first suspicious and watched him for some time. Then seeing nothing unusual in his movements he flew away into the distant sky.

"Nanahboozhoo, in order to carry out his plan to punish the buzzard, resolved to turn himself into a dead deer. He knew that the buzzard lived on dead animals of all kinds. He chose a high spot, visible from a great distance, and there he laid himself down and changed himself into the body of a great deer. It was not long before the various animals and birds that subsist on such things began to gather round this dead body.

"The buzzard, that has such wonderful eyes, to see great distances, saw from afar this gathering of the birds and animals, and as he was ever on the lookout for such things he soon joined the rest of the creatures around the deer. He flew round and round it several times, for he was at first somewhat suspicious. The closest inspection, however, showed him that it was only a dead deer, and that was the unanimous opinion of all the other animals and birds that gathered there. There could be no doubt in any creature's mind but that it was a deer and that it was quite dead.

"The buzzard, now that all his suspicions were gone, in his great greed to get the best he could savagely began, with his powerful beak, tearing a hole in the side of the body that he might get down to the rich fat that is around the kidneys. This is what those fierce, greedy birds always try to get first. Deeper and deeper into the flesh he tore, until at length he was able to crowd in his head and neck to reach the dainty morsels he so much prized.

"This was just what Nanahboozhoo was waiting for, and when the head and neck of the buzzard were completely hidden in the body up jumped the deer, and as he did so the flesh closed up so tightly around the head and neck of the buzzard that the greedy bird was there securely held.

"'Ha, ha, old buzzard! I did catch you after all, as I said I would,' said Nanahboozhoo. 'Now pull out your neck and head.'

"The buzzard with very great difficulty at length succeeded in drawing his head out of the side of the deer. The effort to do so, however, was so great that he lost all of the beautiful feathers that once adorned his head and neck. From that day they have never grown on him again, and there is nothing there to be seen but the red rough-looking skin.

"'Never again,' said Nanahboozhoo, 'will feathers cover your neck or head, and so your friends and enemies, as they see you, will be reminded of how Nanahboozhoo punished you for playing one of your tricks on him. And also from this time forward your food will only be of the rankest kind, and the disagreeable odor will so cling to you that even in the darkest nights your hateful presence will be detected and shunned.'

"Thus," added Souwanas, "the buzzard is the most despised of birds, because he is such an ugly fellow, with his featherless head and neck, and because his disagreeable odor taints the sweet air wherever he goes."

CHAPTER XXIII.

A Moonlight Trip on the Lake--The Legend of the Orphan Boy--His Appeal to the Man in the Moon--How He Conquered His Enemies.

Moonlight nights in the Northland are often very beautiful. There in the summer time the gloaming continues until nearly midnight. Then nothing can be more glorious than to glide along amid the beautiful fir-clad rocky islands in a birch canoe over the still transparent waters. So large and luminous are the full moons of July and August that, with the west aglow and with the wondrous aurora flashing and blazing in the north, there is practically little night and no darkness at all.

Nothing gave the children greater pleasure than to have permission to go with Mary and Kennedy in a large roomy birch canoe for a moonlight excursion during one of those warm, brilliant nights. With plenty of rugs or cushions, to make the coziest of seats in the center of the canoe, they fairly reveled in the beauties of the romantic surroundings while they floated on the moonlit lake. Often in some place of more than ordinary beauty Kennedy would cease paddling, and then their very quietness added to the charms of those happy outings.

"Say, Mary," said Sagastao, "I was reading in one of my books about the 'man in the moon.' Do you know anything about him?"

"He is looking at us very kindly to-night," said Minnehaha. "I really believe I saw him laughing, he is so pleased we have come out to see him this lovely night."

These remarks of the children caused all in the canoe to more closely scan the great round moon that was shining with silvery whiteness straight in front of them.

"There are lots of stories about the moon among our people," said Mary, "but not a great many about the man in the moon. There is, however, a queer one about how he came down and helped a poor orphan boy."

"O, tell it to us just now," said Minnehaha, "while he is watching and listening."

"Do, Mary," said Sagastao, "and Minnehaha and I will watch the old fellow and see how he likes to be talked about."

"Well," said Minnehaha, "Mary will be talking to him to his face, and not behind his back, as people sometimes do when talking about others."

Thus the children ran on with their prattle. Mary and Kennedy were much amused.

"Come, Mary, hurry up! Father said the gloaming would end about eleven, and we must be at the shore by that time."

"Pretty late hours for little children," said Kennedy.

"Never mind that," said Sagastao; "we will make up for it in winter time, when it gets dark at four o'clock."

With Sagastao on one side of her in the big canoe and Minnehaha on the other--their favorite positions when listening to her fascinating stories as she crooned them out in her soft, musical Cree--Mary told them the story.

"Long ago," she began, "there was a poor orphan boy who had neither father nor mother, uncle, aunt, nor any living relative that he knew of. He had a very hard time of it, as the people did not seem to take kindly to him. So he had to live just where he could. He managed to get along all right during the pleasant summer time, but when the long cold winters began he suffered very much. One winter some selfish people let him live with them because he was willing to work hard for what little they did for him. They treated him badly in many ways. They made him go out into the woods and cut firewood, but when he brought it home they would only allow him to stay in the cold entry-way which they had built to their winter dwelling.

"They made him go and hunt different animals for food, and then when he brought, them home they cooked and ate the best themselves, and just threw the fragments and bones to him as they would to a dog. Every member of the household treated him very cruelly, except a nice little girl, the youngest daughter of the family. She felt very sorry for him. She would secretly take him better food, and she furnished him with a knife with which he could cut the tough pieces of meat. She had to be very careful not to be discovered, for if found out she would have been severely punished. So her pity had to show itself on the sly, and the few words she was able to tell him of her sympathy had to be whispered as she passed him, when nobody was looking or listening. The poor boy up to this time had no ambition to better himself, but her kind words and deeds made him resolve that he must begin and do something for himself. But what could he do? Everybody seemed against him but this little girl, and she could do nothing in the way of helping him to escape from these people, who, now that he was becoming so useful to them, would not let him go. What, really, could he do?

"Thus the days and weeks and months passed on and there seemed no chance of escape. He had tried to run away, but had been caught and brought back and beaten.

"One night when it was not very cold he went outside of the narrow entry where he generally had to sleep and threw himself on the ground and cried in his sorrow and despair. He seemed to be utterly unable to better himself. As he lay there he began looking up at the great bright moon that, now so large and round, was, he thought, looking earnestly at him. Soon he was able to see that there was a great man in the moon. As he watched him he was glad to notice that he was not looking crossly at him, but kindly, and so he began crying to the man in the moon to come and help him to escape from the miserable life he was leading. Sure enough, as the boy kept on crying and pleading he saw the man in the moon beginning to come down to this world. He came to the very spot where the unhappy boy was lying, but instead of helping him he made him stand up and then he gave him a good sound thrashing, making the boy, however, strike back at him as vigorously as he could. The beating he got very much disheartened and discouraged the boy, for it was not what he had expected. On the following night, when he had recovered a little, he began reproaching the man in the moon.

"'I called for you,' he said, 'to come and help me against my enemies, and now you have come and thrashed me.'

"But these words, instead of softening the man in the moon, caused him to come down again and give the poor boy a far worse thrashing than before, but for every blow he made the boy return one as good as he had received.

"Now for the first time the boy began to notice that the more he was beaten the stronger he grew. Still he could not understand what the man in the moon meant. So he came again, and they had another regular set-to, and the boy had another good sound thrashing. He asked him what was the meaning of his beating him thus. The man in the moon now spoke to him, but his words were so much like a puzzle that at first the boy did not understand them. This is what the man in the moon said:

"'Would you triumph o'er the strong?
                    Be strong.
       Would you let them no more conquer?
                    Conquer.'

"For a time the boy repeated them over and over. He used to say that as the result of these meetings with the man in the moon he had grown so strong that he was nearly able to hold his own against his antagonist. Then one day, when the man in the moon was puffing from the encounter, the latter said:

"'Now by hard knocks and exercise I have put you on the way of ending your troubles. Be strong, and conquer. Farewell! I am not coming again, as you do not need me any more.'

"Then away he flew back to his place in the moon.

"The boy seemed now to know that he was to use his strength for his own deliverance. To test himself he began tossing up the stones that were so numerous on the shore of the lake. First he began with quite small ones, but soon he found that he could pick up and throw about great big ones, that were like rocks. When he returned from this last contest with the man in the moon it was nearly daylight.

"At first the people began ordering him about as usual. But they soon had reason to be sorry for their cruelty and abuse, for the boy seized one after another of them and flung them with such violence against the rocks that their brains were dashed out and their blood ran in streams down the sides of the rocks--where it turned into seams in the rocks which can be seen to this day.

"One person only, of all who lived in that dwelling, did the now strong boy leave alive, and that was, of course, the good-hearted little girl who used to speak kind words to him and befriend him when she could.

"They grew to be very fond of each other, and were afterward married and lived in full possession of all the things that once belonged to the cruel people for whom the little orphan boy had worked so long."

"Well, sakehou," said Sagastao, "I have been watching the man in the moon while you have been telling the story about his queer way of helping the boy to help himself, and he was looking pleased all the time. So I am sure he is well satisfied with the way you have told the story."

Old Mary was delighted with these words from the lips of the lad she loved with such a passionate devotion.

"But what do you think about it, little sister?" said the lad, calling to Minnehaha, who was cuddled down on the other side of Mary.

But the darling gave no answer, for she had long ago slipped off into Dreamland, and there she remained until the strong arms of Kennedy lifted her up from the canoe and carried her home.

CHAPTER XXIV.

Souwanas's Love for Souwanaquenapeke--How Nanahboozhoo Cured a Little Girl Bitten by a Snake--How the Rattlesnake got Its Rattle--The Origin of Tobacco--Nanahboozhoo in Trouble.

Wahkiegun, as Souwanas named the home of his white friends, always had a warm welcome for Souwanas. Little Souwanaquenapeke had learned to love him and nothing gave the grave old man greater pleasure than to have charge of her for hours at a time. He often carried her away to his wigwam and with great delight explained to visiting Indians how his name was woven into that of the first little paleface born among his people.

Sagastao and Minnehaha, while of course pleased to see the love of the old chief for their sweet little sister, were sometimes a little impatient when they found that he would have his hour with her before they could draw a Nanahboozhoo story out of him.

"You are all right," he would say in his dry, humorous way, "as far as you go; you are only Crees," he would add with a smile, referring to the fact that they had been born among the Cree Indians farther north; "but Souwanaquenapeke is better, as she is a pure Saulteaux."

This of course would put Sagastao and Minnehaha on the defensive, for in those days their own pride of birth was that they were Cree Indians. Faithful old Mary, herself a Cree, would of course take their part, and it was very amusing--laughable at times--to listen to the wordy strife. In these discussions Mary was always the one to first lose her temper. When this happened the penalty was to have the children throw a shawl over her head and thus silence her. From their loving hands she quietly took her punishment and was soon restored to good nature. Good-hearted

Souwanas then speedily responded to the call for a story. But the little Souwanaque-napeke must be, if awake, in his arms, or, if asleep, in a little hammock or native cradle beside him.

"What is it to be about to-day?" asked the old man, as the children, full of eager anticipation, drew a couple of chairs up before him.

After some discussion Souwanas decided to tell them the Nanahboozhoo story of how he lessened the power of the rattlesnakes to do harm.

"Nanahboozhoo, in starting off one day from his grandmother's wigwam, had put on the disguise of a fine young hunter. He had not gone many miles on his journey before he came to a little tent on the edge of the forest where he found a young Indian mother full of grief over her sick child. Nanahboozhoo could not but feel very sorry for her, especially when he heard her story that a snake had crawled noiselessly into her tent and had bitten her little girl while she slept. Nanahboozhoo felt such pity, both for the weeping mother and the bitten child, that at once he set to work to counteract the sad doings of the snake. He hurriedly went into the forest, and there finding a certain plant he said, 'From this day forward the root of this plant shall be a remedy for all people against the bites of snakes.'

"Then Nanahboozhoo showed the mother that the roots were to be pounded and made into a drink and a poultice. The glad mother quickly carried out his instructions and the little girl was soon well again. The Indians have ever since been very thankful to Nanahboozhoo for letting them know of this plant, which they still use for such purposes and which they call snakeroot. Nanahboozhoo remained until he saw that the little girl was quite recovered. Then he said:

"'Now I will fix that snake so that he will not be able to do so much harm in the future.'

"Then going out he caught the king of the snakes and gave him a great scolding for the meanness of that one of his family which had crawled into the tent of the Indian mother and so cruelly bitten that little girl while she slept. Then getting very angry, for Nanahboozhoo was very quick-tempered, he said:

"'Snakes, like other things, have the right to live. They are given their place in the world, and their work. They are to keep down the mice, rats, frogs, toads, and other things that might become too numerous. They have their poisons given them to defend themselves if attacked. But they have no right to go and kill or injure anyone doing them no harm. I'll teach you snakes that in future you cannot quietly crawl about and bite innocent people thus.'

"So he took a piece of the wampum from one of the strings with which he had decorated himself, and having carefully carved the hard shells of which wampum is made, Nanahboozhoo firmly fastened them to the snake's tail, and said:

"'From this day forward may all snakes like you have those noisy rattles upon them, so that all people will call you rattlesnakes. And may it be that you can never move without making a noise with those rattles, so that people will always be able to hear them and thus get ready to fight you, or to get out of your way before you can do any harm.'"

"Well done, Nanahboozhoo!" shouted little Sagastao. "He's the one for me. But why did he not kill all the rattlesnakes at once?"

Souwanas was, however, too clever to be caught trying to answer a question that, although asked by a child, was beyond his knowledge, so he resorted to his calumet, and as the smoke of it began to taint the air Sagastao said, "Well, Souwanas, can you tell us where you Indians first got your tobacco?"

This question was more to the taste of the old Indian, so while he smoked he related the tradition of the introduction of tobacco among his people.

"Very many winters ago," said he, "as Nanahboozhoo was traveling on one of his long journeys he visited a land of great high mountains. One day as he was passing a great chasm in the mountains he saw some blue smoke slowly coming up out of it. This excited his curiosity and he went to see what caused it. As he drew near to it he was very much pleased with its odor. On further investigation he found that the great cave from which the smoke arose was inhabited by a giant who was the keeper of tobacco.

"Nanahboozhoo, on searching, found him half asleep in this cave among great bales and bags of tobacco.

"The smell of the smoke of the tobacco had so pleased Nanahboozhoo that he asked the giant to give him some. The giant refused in a very surly fashion, saying that he only gave portions of it away to his friends the Munedoos, who came once a year to smoke with him.

"Nanahboozhoo, seeing that he was not going to be able to get any by thus pleading for it, snatched up one of the well-filled tobacco bags, dashed out with it, and fled away as rapidly as possible. The great giant was fearfully enraged, and at once began the pursuit of this rash fellow who had thus stolen his tobacco from under his very nose.

"It was a fearful race. Nanahboozhoo had to jump from one mountain top to the next, and so on and on from peak to peak. Closely behind him followed the giant, and Nanahboozhoo had all he could do to keep from being captured. Fortunately for him he now knew the mountains well, and he remembered one ahead of him the opposite side of which was very steep. When he reached this top he suddenly threw himself down upon the very edge, and as the giant passed over him Nanahboozhoo suddenly sprang up and gave him such a push that he tumbled down into the fearful chasm. He was so bruised and wounded that, as he got up and hobbled away down the far-off valley, Nanahboozhoo watching him saw that he looked just like a great grasshopper. He burst out laughing, and then shouted to the giant:

"'For your meanness and selfishness I change you into a grasshopper; Pukaneh shall be your name and you will always have a dirty mouth.'

"And so it is to this day, for every little boy who has caught grasshoppers knows that their saliva is as though they had been chewing tobacco.

"When Nanahboozhoo had rested himself a little he returned to the cave of the giant and took possession of the great quantities of tobacco he found there. He divided it among the Indian tribes, and from that time those who live where it will grow have cultivated it and have supplied all the others."

"I wish," said Minnehaha, "that Nanahboozhoo had left Pukaneh and his tobacco in the cave, for I don't think tobacco smoke is very nice in the house."

Souwanas was amused with the little girl's opposition to his beloved weed, and while she was talking took the opportunity to refill his calumet. When it was in good smoking order he, urgently requested by Sagastao, resumed his story-telling.

"Sometimes it did not fare so well with Nanahboozhoo. There were times when his cleverness seemed to forsake him, and he got into trouble' that at other times he would easily have avoided. For example, one day in the summer time as he was hurrying along he became very thirsty. Soon, however, he came to a river which has many trees on its banks. He pushed his way through them until he came to the bank. Just as he was stooping down to drink he saw some nice ripe fruit in the water. Without seeming to think of what he was doing he dived into the quite shallow water to get the fruit, hit his head against the rocky bottom and was pretty badly hurt. He was vexed and angry as well as disappointed, but he took a good drink of the water and then he lay down on the grass in the shade of the trees to rest. As he lay there on his back he saw above him on the branches of the trees the fruit which he had at first thought was in the water.

"Laughing at his own stupidity and climbing up into the trees he soon had all the ripe fruit he could eat.

"Then on he went, and as his head was quite sore from the bump he had got when he dived into the shallow river he determined to visit some wigwams which he saw not far off.

"The people received him very kindly, with the exception of one surly, cross old man. They quickly prepared some balsam and put it on his wounded head.

"Nanahboozhoo was well pleased with this kindness, and said that he would be glad to perform for them some kindly act in return.

"Before anyone else, however, could speak the cross old man sneered out:

"'O, if you think you are clever enough to do anything, grant that I may live forever!'

"This request and the sneering way in which it was made caused the quick-tempered Nanahboozhoo to become very angry, and he suddenly sprang up and caught the Indian by the shoulders and violently throwing him on the ground said:

"'From this time you shall be a stone, and so your request is granted.'"

CHAPTER XXV.

The Dead Moose--The Rivalry Between the Elk and the Moose People, and Their Various Contests--The Disaster that Befell the Latter Tribe--The Haze of the Indian Summer.

The sight of four stalwart Indians dragging on a dog sled the body of an enormous moose on the ice in front of their home very much interested the children.

Nothing would do but they must be wrapped up and allowed to go out and examine it while the men rested and had a smoke. Its great horns, its enormous ugly head, and then its coarse, bristle-like hair, had all to be examined and commented upon. The opportune arrival of Souwanas, who had been attracted by the sight of the moose, much pleased the children, and just as soon as the investigation of the moose was over and the hunters had proceeded on their journey the children insisted on Souwanas going home to Wahkiegun with them and telling them something about the moose. They also wanted to hear a wonderful story, which he knew, telling how Nanahboozhoo helped the elks to conquer the moose.

When there is a disposition to surrender we are easily conquered. So it was with Souwanas on this occasion. The children in their love for their friend pleaded so importunately that a good cup of tea was prepared for and much enjoyed by him before he began his story, his interested auditors as close as possible around him.

"Once when Nanahboozhoo was journeying through the country," said Souwanas, "he found a village of Indians who were very poor. They were called Oomaskos, Elk people. They had nothing but the poorest of robes on their backs, and they were nearly destitute of everything in the shape of traps, weapons, and canoes. The village was strangely silent, for even the dogs, that generally are around in such numbers, had disappeared. When Nanahboozhoo saw this destitution and poverty he at once inquired the reason, and was surprised and very angry to hear that they were great gamblers.

"Not far off from them was another village whose people were called Mooswa, or Moose people, and Nanahboozhoo soon found out that, while the inhabitants of these two villages were antagonistic to each other, they frequently met to gamble, and that the Moose people were nearly always successful and had won from the Elk people nearly everything they possessed. The latter were very much humiliated at Nanahboozhoo's finding them in such a wretched condition, but they told him they were convinced that some trickery had been practiced upon them by their opponents. They also informed Nanahboozhoo that they would be glad if he would help them to get back their much needed possessions.

"Nanahboozhoo promised that he would assist them on condition that after their possessions were regained they should give up the pernicious habit of gambling. This they unanimously promised to do. The first thing Nanahboozhoo did was to disguise himself as a whisky-jack and fly over to the village of the Moose people and try to discover how it was that they had been so invariably successful when they gambled with the Elk people. It was as he suspected. His old enemies the Anamakquis, the evil spirits that had destroyed his brother Nahpootee, the wolf, had sent one of their number among the Moose people, and he had enabled them to win nearly all of the dogs, as well as other things, from the Elk people. Indeed, he himself had generally been the one who had tossed the plum stones with which they gambled, and they had won by his magic powers.

"When Nanahboozhoo heard this he knew that his first work must be to secure the magic muskamoot (medicine bag). So he flew round and round, and peering in through the top of the wigwam, where the poles crossed each other, he was fortunate enough to see the magic bag hanging up on a cross pole over the place where the Anamakqui slept. He noticed also that it was well guarded and that it would require some cleverness on his part to get it.

"Nanahboozhoo was, as you know, a very clever fellow. He quickly flew back to the village of the Elk people and ordered the most industrious of the women, who were skillful in making fire bags, to make one exactly as he described. This was, of course, similar to the magic muskamoot he had seen hanging up in the tent.

"Nanahboozhoo then put into it things that would have just the opposite effect to those which were in the bag of the Anamakqui. He waited until it was dark, and then, noiselessly flying back to the village of the Moose people, he silently entered the wigwam at the top, where there was now a wide opening, as it was in the warm summer time, very quickly exchanged the bag he had with him for the magic muskamoot, and returned to the village of the Elk people. It did not take him long to arrange his plans. The chief of the Elks had a beautiful daughter, and it was given out that a fine young chief from a far-away tribe had come to ask for her in marriage. The father had welcomed this young chief--who was, of course, Nanahboozhoo--and as he had brought costly gifts he was at once acknowledged as the accepted son-in-law.

"The news spread rapidly and it soon reached the Moose village. When they heard of the many gifts which this rich young stranger had brought with him they, of course, were greedy to win them, as they had won the rest of the Elks' property. It was not many days before a company of them came over to the Elks, and meeting the beautiful daughter of the chief they said:

"'We have come over to have a game of plum stones with your lover, to see if he is a better player than we are.'

"The girl went at once into the wigwam and informed her intended husband, Nanahboozhoo, of the challenge of these people. She also told him that they were very clever but that they had no idea of him being anything else than what he appeared to be. Then she added:

"'Be sure to win; if you do not they will beat us with clubs and sticks. For the custom is that the side that is defeated in the gambling must submit to a beating by the conquerors.'

"Then Nanahboozhoo and the champion for the Moose people sat down on opposite sides of the bowl in which were the plum stones, while the people of each of the two villages ranged themselves behind their own champion. When Nanahboozhoo shook the bowl, and then let the plum stones cease rolling, it was seen that he had won every point. At this the Elks set up a great shout of triumph. The Moose people shouted back:

"'Don't be so fast; the game is to be the best three out of five; just wait until our man has played.'

"The plum stones were then handed to him and patting his medicine bag he confidently shook them up, but when they had ceased rolling it was seen that he had lost every point.

"The victory was now so nearly won that the Elks began to say:

"'Get your clubs ready to thrash the Moose people, for we are surely going to be winners this day.'

"The Moose people were, however, not yet quite discouraged. 'There are three tries yet,' they said, 'and our man may yet win.' But their hopes were soon gone, for when Nanahboozhoo threw the plum stones the third time he was as successful as at the first.

"This decided the game in favor of the Elks, who now rushed upon the Moose people and thrashed them all the way back to their own village.

"The Moose were very much humiliated at this defeat. They had not only had a good beating but, according to the custom of the tribes, they were obliged to restore much of the property which they had won from the Elks in their previous contests. A council was called not long after and there was quite a discussion among them as to the best plan to be adopted to defeat the Elks and regain supremacy. They decided on a trial of strength, for in such encounters they had generally been victorious. They had two high poles erected with a crossbar on the top, and the contest was to see which side could produce the man who should throw the heaviest stone over that bar. They sent their challenge to the Elks to meet them if they dare.

"The Elks quickly responded and were soon at the place where the Moose people, who were awaiting them, had erected the high poles with the crossbar. When everything had been arranged their strongest man took up a heavy stone and, with a tremendous effort, succeeded in barely throwing it, so that it struck the crossbar and carried it down to the ground. When the crossbar had been replaced a son of the chief of the Elks went forward, as though he would be the competitor on the side of the Elks. He pretended as though he could not even lift the heavy stone which the Moose champion had thrown. When the Moose people saw this they shouted out in triumph, and began to get ready to give the Elks as good a beating as they had received from them on a former occasion.

"Seeing them thus coming, Nanahboozhoo rushed forward, seized the heavy stone, and sent it high up and far over the tops of the poles--thus winning the victory again for the Elks. With a shout of triumph the Elks again attacked the Moose and drove them in disgrace back to their own village. The Moose people were now more humiliated than ever, but they determined to try another plan; for they were resolved not to give up to the Elks, whom they had so often defeated. After much consultation they said:

"'Let us have a contest at diving in the lake, that we may see if our champion cannot remain longer under the water than any one of the Elks.'

"So they went over to the village of the Elks and told them they had come to have another contest with them. To the proposal of the Moose the Elks all agreed, and both parties proceeded to the lake. Here a large hole was cut in the ice and the champion of the Moose prepared to go down into the water. One of the brothers of the beautiful Indian girl who had been selected as Nanahboozhoo's bride said to Nanahboozhoo:

"'As our bodies are tougher than yours you must let me compete this time.'

"Nanahboozhoo would not let him do this. He said:

"'I am not afraid of the cold water, and besides I have plenty of friends down there.'

"And, sure enough, the mud turtle came up and said, in words that only Nanahboozhoo could understand:

"'My brother, I have come up at the request of your brother, the wolf, to aid you. Trust yourself in my care and no harm will come to you.'

"Nanahboozhoo was well pleased to hear this, for he knew that his spirit brother had sent his friend the mud turtle to help him in this trial.

"The competitors now stripped themselves, and when the signal was given they both dived into the water and disappeared. The Moose people had such confidence in their champion that they had all brought with them very heavy sticks with which they intended giving the Elks a great beating in return for the two previous defeats.

"The Elks, however, were not dismayed. They only said:

"'Just wait until the contest is decided.'

"In the meantime the competitors under the water were so near together at first that the people on the land heard the Moose say, 'Elk, are you cold?' To which the mud turtle, who had covered the Elk competitor over with his shell, replied:

"'No, Moose; but are you cold?'

"As the people on the shore could not hear any answer to this question it gave some alarm to the Moose people about their champion, who they feared must be benumbed with the cold. This was really the case, for in a short time he came to the surface of the water so nearly frozen to death that he had to be helped out of the water.

"When the mud turtle and Nanahboozhoo heard the shoutings of triumph of the Elks they knew that the Moose champion had failed, and so they came up to the surface. Nanahboozhoo swam ashore and joined in the pursuit of the disheartened Moose people, who had again so signally failed.

"These repeated defeats very much angered and humiliated the Moose people. They almost quarreled among themselves in their vexation as they talked them over at their councils. Still they were in no humor to give up. They had two very swift runners among them, and they decided to challenge the Elks to a foot race. So they again sent a number of their party over to the tent of the Elk people and said:

"'We are not at all satisfied yet, and we wish to know if the son of the chief and his brother-in-law, the young stranger who has come into your midst, will run a foot race against two of our young people.'

"This challenge was at once accepted and soon all preparations were made for the great race. It was decided that it should be run on the ice of the frozen lake, which was several miles round. Much snow had fallen, but the people of both sides turned out for days and cleared out a good track. They made it near the shore, and so that the finishing spot would be near where was the starting point.

"The Moose felt quite certain of winning this time, because by their magic their runners were to be turned into real Moose, with four legs, and they argued that runners with four feet could surely beat those who had only two. But there were others who had heard about this great race, and among them was the wolf, the spirit brother of Nanahboozhoo, and so he came to him the night before the race.

"'My brother,' he said, 'I will come and help you in this race. You are the only one that can see me, so I will be on the track, about half way round, and when you come there you can get on my back and I will carry you at a greater speed. But you must keep your legs moving as if rapidly running, or the people will suspect something unusual.'

"There was a great crowd to witness this race between the two great Moose, to represent the Moose people, and the son of the chief and his unknown brother-in-law to represent the Elks. When the signal was given away they started over the icy trail. The Moose soon were at the front, with the chief's son not far behind. Nanahboozhoo was purposely a little in the rear, and so was able to spring upon the wolf's back without attracting attention.

"With this steed under him he sped along with marvelous rapidity. At the half-way point of the race he overtook his brother-in-law, and giving him his hand, they were soon far in front. When they rushed in ahead there was great excitement. The Moose people were soon running back to their village with the Elks whipping them to the very doors of their wigwams.

"After this the Moose dare not challenge the Elks to any further contest, but they were so furious that they meditated murder in their hearts toward the young stranger, who had, they now saw, been the cause of their many defeats. Nanahboozhoo, however, easily thwarted their evil schemes, but at length some of them were so bad that his anger was aroused and he exerted all his magic power.

"'Moose you are by name,' he said to them, 'and for your bad deeds I change you into the animals after whom you are named. Hereafter you will live in the swamps, among the willows and young birch. On them you will have to browse for a living. For a little variety in your food you may, in the summer time, go out into the shallow waters and paw up and eat the great roots of the water-lilies.'

"Thus the Elks again had peace and quietness. Gambling was never again allowed among them, and Nanahboozhoo, after receiving their grateful thanks, returned to his own country."

"What did he do after that?" asked Sagastao.

"Not much, for a while; but after a time he decided to go away up North. Each fall, however, he comes and looks around to see how everything is going on. Then he rests on some of the mountains and has a big smoke, which settles down on the hillsides and valleys and makes the beautiful hazy time which we all call the Indian Summer."

"Well," said Minnehaha, "if the smoke of Nanahboozhoo's big pipe of peace makes the beautiful haze of the lovely Indian Summer, it is about the best thing I have heard yet of tobacco smoke doing."

And so say we all.

GLOSSARY

Ana-mak-qui, ***Evil spirits or magicians***.

An-nun-gi-tee, ***The ghost with big ears***.

Ja-koos, ***Strong-armed***.

Keche-Wapoose, ***Great Rabbit***.

Kin-ne-sa-sis, ***Little Fish***.

Kosh-ke-e-wa-see, ***Partridge***.

Ma-hei-gan, ***Wolf***.

Mani-boos or Manitoos or Munedoos, ***Spirits***.

Me-squah-be-me-sheen, ***Red Willows***.

Minne-ha-ha, ***Laughing Waters***.

Mis-ta-coo-sis, ***Aspen Tree***.

Mis-mis, ***Grandfather***.

Moos-wa, ***Moose***.

Moo-she-kin-ne-bik, ***Sea Monster***.

Musk-a-moot, ***Medicine Bag***.

Mud-je-kee-wis, ***West Wind***.

Na-nah-booz-hoo, ***Son of Mud-je-kee-wis--West Wind***.

Nah-poo-tee, ***Wolf***.

Ni-koo-chis, ***Solitude--name of a giant***.

Nokomis, ***Grandmother***.

Ome-mee, ***Pigeon or Dove***.

Oo-kis-ki-mu-ni-sew, ***Kingfisher***.

Oo-see-mee-id, ***The Younger***.

Se-si-giz-it, *The Older*.

Pa-peu-pe-na-ses, ***Laughing Bird***.

Pug-a-mah-kon, ***A hammer***.

Puk-an-eh, ***Grasshopper***.

Sa-gas-ta-oo-ke-mou, shortened to Sagastao, ***The Sunrise Gentleman***.

Sa-ke-how, ***Beloved***.

Se-se-pask-wut, ***Sugar***.

Sis-tin-a-koo, ***The magician who guarded the fire in the interior of the earth***.

Shu-ni-ou, ***Money***.

So-qua-a-tum, ***Steadfast***.

Sou-wa-nas, ***South Wind, The great Story-teller***.

Sou-wa-na-que-na-peke, ***The Voice of the South Wind Birds***.

Wah-ki-e-gun, ***The House***.

Wau-be-noo, ***The East***.

Wakonda, ***A supernatural Person***.

Wakontas, ***Son of Wakonda***.

Wau-konug, ***Lichen***.

Wenonah, ***Daughter of Nokomis and mother of Nanahboozhoo***.

The Codes Of Hammurabi And Moses
W. W. Davies

QTY

The discovery of the Hammurabi Code is one of the greatest achievements of archaeology, and is of paramount interest, not only to the student of the Bible, but also to all those interested in ancient history...

Religion   ISBN: *1-59462-338-4*   Pages:132
MSRP $12.95

The Theory of Moral Sentiments
Adam Smith

QTY

This work from 1749. contains original theories of conscience amd moral judgment and it is the foundation for systemof morals.

Philosophy ISBN: *1-59462-777-0*   Pages:536
MSRP $19.95

Jessica's First Prayer
Hesba Stretton

QTY

In a screened and secluded corner of one of the many railway-bridges which span the streets of London there could be seen a few years ago, from five o'clock every morning until half past eight, a tidily set-out coffee-stall, consisting of a trestle and board, upon which stood two large tin cans, with a small fire of charcoal burning under each so as to keep the coffee boiling during the early hours of the morning when the work-people were thronging into the city on their way to their daily toil...

Childrens   ISBN: *1-59462-373-2*   Pages:84
MSRP $9.95

My Life and Work
Henry Ford

QTY

Henry Ford revolutionized the world with his implementation of mass production for the Model T automobile. Gain valuable business insight into his life and work with his own auto-biography... "We have only started on our development of our country we have not as yet, with all our talk of wonderful progress, done more than scratch the surface. The progress has been wonderful enough but..."

Biographies/   ISBN: *1-59462-198-5*   Pages:300
MSRP $21.95

The Art of Cross-Examination
Francis Wellman

QTY

I presume it is the experience of every author, after his first book is published upon an important subject, to be almost overwhelmed with a wealth of ideas and illustrations which could readily have been included in his book, and which to his own mind, at least, seem to make a second edition inevitable. Such certainly was the case with me; and when the first edition had reached its sixth impression in five months, I rejoiced to learn that it seemed to my publishers that the book had met with a sufficiently favorable reception to justify a second and considerably enlarged edition. ..

Pages:412

Reference   **ISBN:** *1-59462-647-2*   *MSRP $19.95*

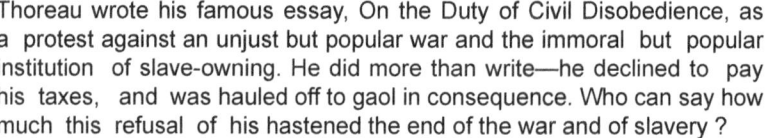

On the Duty of Civil Disobedience
Henry David Thoreau

QTY

Thoreau wrote his famous essay, On the Duty of Civil Disobedience, as a protest against an unjust but popular war and the immoral but popular institution of slave-owning. He did more than write—he declined to pay his taxes,   and was hauled off to gaol in consequence. Who can say how much this refusal of his hastened the end of the war and of slavery ?

Law   **ISBN:** *1-59462-747-9*   **Pages:48**

MSRP $7.45

Dream Psychology Psychoanalysis for Beginners
Sigmund Freud

QTY

Sigmund Freud, born Sigismund Schlomo Freud (May 6, 1856 - September 23, 1939), was a Jewish-Austrian neurologist and psychiatrist who co-founded the psychoanalytic school of psychology. Freud is best known for his theories of the unconscious mind, especially involving the mechanism of repression; his redefinition of sexual desire as mobile and directed towards a wide variety of objects; and his therapeutic techniques, especially his understanding of transference in the therapeutic relationship and the presumed value of dreams as sources of insight into unconscious desires.

Dream Psychology
Psychoanalysis for Beginners

Sigmund Freud

Pages:196

Psychology   **ISBN:** *1-59462-905-6*   *MSRP $15.45*

The Miracle of Right Thought
Orison Swett Marden

QTY

Believe with all of your heart that you will do what you were made to do. When the mind has once formed the habit of holding cheerful, happy, prosperous pictures, it will not be easy to form the opposite habit. It does not matter how improbable or how far away this realization may see, or how dark the prospects may be, if we visualize them as best we can, as vividly as possible, hold tenaciously to them and vigorously struggle to attain them, they will gradually become actualized, realized in the life. But a desire, a longing without endeavor, a yearning abandoned or held indifferently will vanish without realization.

Pages:360

Self Help   **ISBN:** *1-59462-644-8*   *MSRP $25.45*

QTY

The Rosicrucian Cosmo-Conception Mystic Christianity *by Max Heindel*   ISBN: 1-59462-188-8   **$38.95**
The Rosicrucian Cosmo-conception is not dogmatic, neither does it appeal to any other authority than the reason of the student. It is: not controversial, but is: sent forth in the, hope that it may help to clear...   New Age/Religion Pages 646

Abandonment To Divine Providence *by Jean-Pierre de Caussade*   ISBN: 1-59462-228-0   **$25.95**
"The Rev. Jean Pierre de Caussade was one of the most remarkable spiritual writers of the Society of Jesus in France in the 18th Century. His death took place at Toulouse in 1751. His works have gone through many editions and have been republished...   Inspirational/Religion Pages 400

Mental Chemistry *by Charles Haanel*   ISBN: 1-59462-192-6   **$23.95**
Mental Chemistry allows the change of material conditions by combining and appropriately utilizing the power of the mind. Much like applied chemistry creates something new and unique out of careful combinations of chemicals the mastery of mental chemistry...   New Age Pages 354

The Letters of Robert Browning and Elizabeth Barret Barrett 1845-1846 vol II   ISBN: 1-59462-193-4   **$35.95**
by Robert Browning and Elizabeth Barrett   Biographies Pages 596

Gleanings In Genesis (volume I) *by Arthur W. Pink*   ISBN: 1-59462-130-6   **$27.45**
Appropriately has Genesis been termed "the seed plot of the Bible" for in it we have, in germ form, almost all of the great doctrines which are afterwards fully developed in the books of Scripture which follow...   Religion/Inspirational Pages 420

The Master Key *by L. W. de Laurence*   ISBN: 1-59462-001-6   **$30.95**
In no branch of human knowledge has there been a more lively increase of the spirit of research during the past few years than in the study of Psychology, Concentration and Mental Discipline. The requests for authentic lessons in Thought Control, Mental Discipline and...   New Age/Business Pages 422

The Lesser Key Of Solomon Goetia *by L. W. de Laurence*   ISBN: 1-59462-092-X   **$9.95**
This translation of the first book of the "Lernegton" which is now for the first time made accessible to students of Talismanic Magic was done, after careful collation and edition, from numerous Ancient Manuscripts in Hebrew, Latin, and French...   New Age/Occult Pages 92

Rubaiyat Of Omar Khayyam *by Edward Fitzgerald*   ISBN:1-59462-332-5   **$13.95**
Edward Fitzgerald, whom the world has already learned, in spite of his own efforts to remain within the shadow of anonymity, to look upon as one of the rarest poets of the century, was born at Bredfield, in Suffolk, on the 31st of March, 1809. He was the third son of John Purcell...   Music Pages 172

Ancient Law *by Henry Maine*   ISBN: 1-59462-128-4   **$29.95**
The chief object of the following pages is to indicate some of the earliest ideas of mankind, as they are reflected in Ancient Law, and to point out the relation of those ideas to modern thought.   Religiom/History Pages 452

Far-Away Stories *by William J. Locke*   ISBN: 1-59462-129-2   **$19.45**
"Good wine needs no bush, but a collection of mixed vintages does. And this book is just such a collection. Some of the stories I do not want to remain buried for ever in the museum files of dead magazine-numbers an author's not unpardonable vanity..."   Fiction Pages 272

Life of David Crockett *by David Crockett*   ISBN: 1-59462-250-7   **$27.45**
"Colonel David Crockett was one of the most remarkable men of the times in which he lived. Born in humble life, but gifted with a strong will, an indomitable courage, and unremitting perseverance...   Biographies/New Age Pages 424

Lip-Reading *by Edward Nitchie*   ISBN: 1-59462-206-X   **$25.95**
Edward B. Nitchie, founder of the New York School for the Hard of Hearing, now the Nitchie School of Lip-Reading, Inc, wrote "LIP-READING Principles and Practice". The development and perfecting of this meritorious work on lip-reading was an undertaking...   How-to Pages 400

A Handbook of Suggestive Therapeutics, Applied Hypnotism, Psychic Science   ISBN: 1-59462-214-0   **$24.95**
by Henry Munro   Health/New Age/Health/Self-help Pages 376

A Doll's House: and Two Other Plays *by Henrik Ibsen*   ISBN: 1-59462-112-8   **$19.95**
Henrik Ibsen created this classic when in revolutionary 1848 Rome. Introducing some striking concepts in playwriting for the realist genre, this play has been studied the world over.   Fiction/Classics/Plays 308

The Light of Asia *by sir Edwin Arnold*   ISBN: 1-59462-204-3   **$13.95**
In this poetic masterpiece, Edwin Arnold describes the life and teachings of Buddha. The man who was to become known as Buddha to the world was born as Prince Gautama of India but he rejected the worldly riches and abandoned the reigns of power when...   Religion/History/Biographies Pages 170

The Complete Works of Guy de Maupassant *by Guy de Maupassant*   ISBN: 1-59462-157-8   **$16.95**
"For days and days, nights and nights, I had dreamed of that first kiss which was to consecrate our engagement, and I knew not on what spot I should put my lips..."   Fiction/Classics Pages 240

The Art of Cross-Examination *by Francis L. Wellman*   ISBN: 1-59462-309-0   **$26.95**
Written by a renowned trial lawyer, Wellman imparts his experience and uses case studies to explain how to use psychology to extract desired information through questioning.   How-to/Science/Reference Pages 408

Answered or Unanswered? *by Louisa Vaughan*   ISBN: 1-59462-248-5   **$10.95**
Miracles of Faith in China   Religion Pages 112

The Edinburgh Lectures on Mental Science (1909) *by Thomas*   ISBN: 1-59462-008-3   **$11.95**
This book contains the substance of a course of lectures recently given by the writer in the Queen Street Hall, Edinburgh. Its purpose is to indicate the Natural Principles governing the relation between Mental Action and Material Conditions...   New Age/Psychology Pages 148

Ayesha *by H. Rider Haggard*   ISBN: 1-59462-301-5   **$24.95**
Verily and indeed it is the unexpected that happens! Probably if there was one person upon the earth from whom the Editor of this, and of a certain previous history, did not expect to hear again...   Classics Pages 380

Ayala's Angel *by Anthony Trollope*   ISBN: 1-59462-352-X   **$29.95**
The two girls were both pretty, but Lucy who was twenty-one who supposed to be simple and comparatively unattractive, whereas Ayala was credited, as her Bombwhat romantic name might show, with poetic charm and a taste for romance. Ayala when her father died was nineteen...   Fiction Pages 484

The American Commonwealth *by James Bryce*   ISBN: 1-59462-286-8   **$34.45**
An interpretation of American democratic political theory. It examines political mechanics and society from the perspective of Scotsman James Bryce   Politics Pages 572

Stories of the Pilgrims *by Margaret P. Pumphrey*   ISBN: 1-59462-116-2   **$17.95**
This book explores pilgrims religious oppression in England as well as their escape to Holland and eventual crossing to America on the Mayflower, and their early days in New England...   History Pages 268

QTY

The Fasting Cure *by Sinclair Upton*   ISBN: *1-59462-222-1*   **$13.95**   ☐
In the Cosmopolitan Magazine for May, 1910, and in the Contemporary Review (London) for April, 1910, I published an article dealing with my experiences in fasting. I have written a great many magazine articles, but never one which attracted so much attention... New Age/Self Help/Health Pages 164

Hebrew Astrology *by Sepharial*   ISBN: *1-59462-308-2*   **$13.45**   ☐
In these days of advanced thinking it is a matter of common observation that we have left many of the old landmarks behind and that we are now pressing forward to greater heights and to a wider horizon than that which represented the mind-content of our progenitors... Astrology Pages 144

Thought Vibration or The Law of Attraction in the Thought World   ISBN: *1-59462-127-6*   **$12.95**   ☐
by William Walker Atkinson   Psychology/Religion Pages 144

Optimism *by Helen Keller*   ISBN: *1-59462-108-X*   **$15.95**   ☐
Helen Keller was blind, deaf, and mute since 19 months old, yet famously learned how to overcome these handicaps, communicate with the world, and spread her lectures promoting optimism. An inspiring read for everyone... Biographies/Inspirational Pages 84

Sara Crewe *by Frances Burnett*   ISBN: *1-59462-360-0*   **$9.45**   ☐
In the first place, Miss Minchin lived in London. Her home was a large, dull, tall one, in a large, dull square, where all the houses were alike, and all the sparrows were alike, and where all the door-knockers made the same heavy sound... Childrens/Classic Pages 88

The Autobiography of Benjamin Franklin *by Benjamin Franklin*   ISBN: *1-59462-135-7*   **$24.95**   ☐
The Autobiography of Benjamin Franklin has probably been more extensively read than any other American historical work, and no other book of its kind has had such ups and downs of fortune. Franklin lived for many years in England, where he was agent... Biographies/History Pages 332

Name	
Email	
Telephone	
Address	
City, State ZIP	

☐ **Credit Card**   ☐ **Check / Money Order**

Credit Card Number	
Expiration Date	
Signature	

Please Mail to: Book Jungle
                          PO Box 2226
                          Champaign, IL 61825
or Fax to: 630-214-0564

ORDERING INFORMATION

web*: www.bookjungle.com*
email*: sales@bookjungle.com*
fax*: 630-214-0564*
mail*: Book Jungle PO Box 2226 Champaign, IL 61825*
or PayPal *to sales@bookjungle.com*

Please contact us for bulk discounts

DIRECT-ORDER TERMS

**20% Discount if You Order
Two or More Books**
Free Domestic Shipping!
Accepted: Master Card, Visa,
Discover, American Express

www.ingramcontent.com/pod-product-compliance
Lightning Source LLC
Chambersburg PA
CBHW080908020726

47502CB00008B/2390

* 9 7 8 1 4 3 8 5 3 2 9 5 0 *